Edward Cooper Willis

Tales and Legends in Verse

Edward Cooper Willis

Tales and Legends in Verse

ISBN/EAN: 9783337174194

Printed in Europe, USA, Canada, Australia, Japan

Cover: Foto ©Andreas Hilbeck / pixelio.de

More available books at **www.hansebooks.com**

TALES AND LEGENDS

IN VERSE

E. COOPER WILLIS, Q.C.

LONDON

KEGAN PAUL, TRENCH & CO., 1, PATERNOSTER SQUARE

1888

CONTENTS.

SHORT PIECES.

TALES AND LEGENDS
IN VERSE.

THE CHAIN OF GOLD.

THE snow lay heavy on heath and bush, and the path
    was hard to find,
Fierce and bitter the sleet and hail on the gusts of
    the frozen wind;
Dim and grey through the drifting haze the light was
    failing fast,
And the wail as of a dying year was borne upon the
    blast.
Sick at heart, with surging thoughts and doubts far
    worse than pain,
The young man slowly fought his way across the
    broken plain,
Until the storm that howled around had beaten the
    storm of the mind,
And in the very struggle for life his doubts were cast
    behind.

B

Slow, slow, with stumbling foot, o'er hillock, hollow,
    and stone,
With the death-chill driving through the breath and
    piercing to the bone,
Through the drifting storm with labouring heart and
    faint and blinded eye,
Till there almost seemed no end at last but to lie
    down and die,
Until the will that had borne him up half yielded to
    despair,
And the lips that long had lost their God gasped
    feebly in a prayer,
He struggled on. Hope came again. The battle
    was renewed :
Step by step he fought his way, defied, but unsub-
    dued ;
And it seemed an answer to the prayer—the slacken-
    ing of the gale ;
And its howling dropped to a murmur, and lighter fell
    the hail.

But deep the drifts, and far the end, and he was
    weary of fight ;
And o'er the drear expanse there fell the shadows of
    the night :
When close beside his path he saw a motion in the
    snow,
And he heard the sound as of a sob, fluttering, feeble,
    and low.

It came from beneath the shroud on the earth; and
    something—he knew not what—
Bore down the hard stern self in his heart, and turned
    him to the spot.
And there, beneath the frozen wreath, he found them
    side by side,
A little, scarcely living child, a mother who had died.
Her mantle wrapped around the babe, she laid it on
    her breast,
And, giving all to save her all, she passed away to
    rest.

Again was heard the pleading cry, the little hand was
    raised,
And feelings all unknown before came o'er him as he
    gazed,
And he seemed to have gained a heart of flesh instead
    of a heart of stone,
As he took the child from the breast of the dead, and
    laid it in his own,
And closed it from the cold, and sought to soothe its
    moaning pain,
And, in the new-born strength of love, tried the dark
    path again.

The end was far and the drifts were deep, but the
    storm had passed away;
And, softly sleeping, at his heart the little orphan lay;
And through the lifted clouds one star sent down its
    tiny ray.

Onward he went, and, as he went, there shone before
    his eye,
Outbursting from the failing cloud, the glories of the
    sky;
And firmly, slowly, lightened by the precious load he
    bore,
O'er hillock, hollow, and stone he passed, and gained
    the welcome door.
But, as he passed the village church, the window's
    painted glow
Lay like a picture in his path upon the gleaming
    snow:
Weary, but victor, stained with blood, in colours fair
    to see,
The Shepherd and the rescued lamb; the motto,
    " Follow Me."

A few short days, the little life just flickered for a
    while.
She learnt to look for his return, to brighten at his
    smile;
And as he kissed the withered cheek or smoothed the
    clustered hair,
Would turn to nestle in his arm, and find a refuge
    there;
And wreathed her love around his heart, until the
    fairy chain
So strong had grown, no power of life might wrest its
    folds in twain.

It was the holy Christmas Eve.   He watched her as
    she lay,
Till the flush on the cheek and the fevered start in
    sleep had passed away.
The lingering hours wore slowly on, the fire was
    burning low,
And the dim shadows on the wall were wavering to
    and fro.
Perchance he slept.   Before his soul a vision seemed
    to rise—
No brighter, truer sight was e'er vouchsafed to mortal
    eyes.
The bells had pealed the midnight chime, 'twas
    Christmas in the land,
When he was aware of an angel fair who touched him
    with her hand.
He rose obedient to the touch, and followed where
    she led.
The flowers of heaven burst from earth beneath the
    angel's tread.
She pointed where the glorious stars were scattered
    far and wide,
And, like a mist before the wind, she vanished from
    his side.
And as he gazed upon the sky those glories brighter
    grew—
O'er the deep tones of the winter night there spread a
    golden hue ;

The heavens were filled with angel forms that, bending
 o'er the earth,
Poured the full notes of that sweet song that hailed
 the Saviour's birth.
And one, in likeness of a child,—he knew that face
 again,
All radiant now, released at last from weakness and
 from pain,—
Flew down and touched his hands and lips with
 kisses soft and light,
And softly whispering, " Follow me ! " she passed,
 and it was night.

Then with a start he woke. The hand he held within
 his fold
Returned no pressure to his grasp. 'Twas lifeless all,
 and cold.
A light. So gently o'er the heart had passed the hand
 of death,
It seemed as though an angel's lips had kissed away
 her breath.

The old man lay on the bed of pain, and the years
 that had gone by—
The years that once had been his friends, came round
 to see him die.
Blotted and blurred their outlines, sad were the tales
 they told ;

But they all seemed linked together, as it were with
    a chain of gold.
And the chain went back in the distance till it came
    to the long ago,
When the young man bent o'er the little child lost in
    the wreath of snow ;
And since that night, as following years brought back
    the Christmas-tide,
Each Christmas morn had brought again that angel
    to his side,
Had sung for him the song of love, the kiss of love
    had given,
And added a link to the chain of gold that bound his
    soul to heaven.
The blessed vision aye returned with bright and
    brighter glow,
And in his inmost heart he knew the bidding sweet
    and low,
And saw the Shepherd and the lamb upon the gleam-
    ing snow.

Now, old and worn, with feeble heart, he laid him
    down to die ;
The shadows wavered on the wall before his filming
    eye ;
The bells had chimed the midnight hour, 'twas
    Christmas in the land,
When he was aware of an angel fair who touched him
    with her hand.

He rose obedient to the touch, and followed where
she led,
The flowers of heaven burst from earth beneath the
angel's tread.
And as he waited for the end, outburst the blessèd
song,
And he saw the haloed light that spread around the
heavenly throng;
He saw the spirit of the child descending like a dove;
He felt the arms encircling round, he felt the kiss of
love;
He heard the blessèd "Welcome home!" and hand
in hand they went
Up to the heaven of heavens, beyond the starry
firmament.
The worn and weary frame was dead; but ere the
heart grew cold,
Within the treasure-house of God blazed the bright
chain of gold.

TYRRELL'S CONFESSION

(ORIGINALLY INSERTED IN "TEMPLE BAR MAGAZINE," 1869.)

On the morrow after Lammas Day in the last year of the eleventh century, William, the king, was slain by an arrow from his own men in the New Forest, and was carried to Winchester and buried there. Such in effect is the tale of the old Saxon chronicle. No bell, we are told, was rung for him; no mass sung for the repose of his soul; but he was buried like a wild beast, unwept and unhonoured. To make that forest his father had wasted fields, and driven into misery and death the tillers of the soil, for over a space of thirty miles in length. There his brother Richard had years before met with a sudden and mysterious death. There William himself had enforced all the cruelties of the forest laws, and men had had their eyes scorched out, or lost their lives, for sacrilegiously interfering with the game which the king delighted to honour; and there, near a ruined church, he fell, smitten, as it was thought, by the wrath of God through the hand of man. Many were the tales of warnings sent of the coming fate. Dreams and messages were in vain, and if the king believed them at all, he hid his belief under a bold face.

On that 2nd of August he was at his hunting-lodge at Brockenhurst. Amongst his companions was Sir Walter Tyrrell, or "the Archer," Lord of Poix in Ponthieu and of a small barony

in Essex.   As the company sat over their meal, words spoken at
first in jest culminated in bitterness, until the boasting threats of
the king rankled in the heart of his follower.   Then were brought
in before William six shafts for the crossbow, and he, choosing
two, handed them to Tyrrell to be used in the chase, bidding
him do justice with them.   " I will do so," was the significant
reply, and soon afterwards the whole party mounted and pro-
ceeded into the forest.   It is said that the rest of the hunters
went in other directions, and that William and Tyrrell rode
alone.   Then, as the autumn sun was setting, the bleeding body
of the king was found pierced by one of the shafts, and was
carried on a labourer's cart to Winchester.

Tyrrell was seen no more in England.   He escaped to France,
and common tradition has pointed him out as the slayer of his
lord.   Some chronicles state that the death was caused by an
accident from the glancing of the arrow from a tree.   Tyrrell
himself is reported to have stated that he was not near William
when he fell, but whether this report is true or not, the facts
remain that he was believed to have done the deed, that he
fled away, and that he never returned to England or attempted
to recover the profits from his English lands.   It is, of course,
possible that some other hand may have been guilty, and that
the outcry against Tyrrell was raised in order to conceal the
real culprit.   On the other hand, it is equally possible and
more probable that the charge was based not only on his own
conduct, but also on knowledge of the quarrel which had taken
place on the very day of the murder.   Neither fearing God nor
regarding man, the coarse brutality of the king must often have
deeply offended those who were drawn around him by motives
of self-interest, and it is easy to imagine how the fierce French-
man may have brooded over the last of many insults, and de-
termined to avenge all in one fatal blow.   And so, in the forest
consecrated to bloodshed, the tyrant's soul passed away.   The
murderer might for a time deny the accusation or attempt to
explain it away ; but when the spirit that nerved the hand had
itself grown feeble, and the time drew near that he must die,

anxious to obtain the last ministrations of the Church, he would, in the depth of self-abasement, confess the truth, and acknowledge the weight with which the crime had for all those years been pressing upon him.

FATHER, I cannot pass away,
    I linger as I lie;
For the wrath of God keeps life within.
Oh, shrive me, and let me go free from my sin !
    Bless me, and let me die.

Father, it's thirty years ago,
    A weary chain of years,
When the worn heart seeks in vain for grace,
And the great God turns away His face,
    And there's no relief in tears.

Fearful the past; the present—hell;
    The future all unknown.
I did not even dare to die :
And we have lived, the curse and I,
    Together and alone.

If it had been but in the fight,
    When hand's opposed to hand,
Had I but sought him as a foe,
Met thrust with thrust, and blow with blow,
    And slain him with my brand,

I had not deemed his death a sin,
    Nor mourned a single day ;
But, oh ! it is a fearful crime
To wait for an unguarded time,
    And then take life away.

He was my king and feudal lord,
    He gave me lands in fee ;
And God and the holy saints, they heard
When I swore to be true in deed and word,
    As I bent before his knee.

I swore to be true in deed and word,
    And surely I meant it then ;
But it's hard to keep, though easy to say,
And time was long, and I went astray,
    Even as other men.

Perchance it was but a jeering word—
    A look—some trivial slight,—
I cannot tell ; I never knew
When it began, or how it grew—
    A dark and fearful blight,

The deadly curse of thwarted pride,
    The blight of a hating soul ;
And ever it led me on and on,
Till pity and Christian love were gone,
    And murder was the goal.

But I held my thought within my breast,
    And I could fawn and smile ;
And still I took the gifts he gave—
Took them, and felt myself a slave—
    And cursed him all the while.

All thoughts were gone, save the constant thought
    Of only how and when ;
And as time went on, I laid my plan—
I had been more or less than man
    If I had wavered then.

We were together in the wood,
    Hunting the fallow deer ;
He rode before me like a king,
I, as a slave, was following,
    And there was no one near.

And a mist rose up before my eyes,
    A tumult in my brain ;
And, swifter than a startled deer,
The pulses rushed in mad career
    Through every swollen vein.

I could not hear the wind in the trees,
    I could not see the light,
For the blood that boiled like flames in hell,
For the sound of death, like a 'larum bell,
    Rung on a wintry night.

A moment—and again the heart
    Beat in its own control ;
And the brain knew nought but the living will,
The steadfast deep resolve to kill,
    The hatred of the soul.

I held my breath and kept it still ;
    My sight was clear as day ;
My pulse was quiet as the dead.
I drew an arrow to the head,
    And launched it forth to slay.

I marked each second of its flight ;
    I saw it pierce his side :
'Twas but a grapple at the rein,
A plunging fall, a writhe of pain.
    And so the Red King died.

I do not know how others feel
    Who do as I have done ;
Who fear, yet plan the deed of strife,
Then find the object of a life
    In one short murder won :

I felt no change, yet change there was—
    I could not hate the dead ;
I rode to where the body lay—
That silent, bleeding mass of clay
    Woke neither grief nor dread.

I only felt I must away,
    To hide the murderer's head.

Away! and in the rush of flight,
    I banished, for a time,
All that I felt and all I saw,
The vision of a broken law,
    The memory of crime.

'Twas only for a little while—
    A little, oh! so brief;
For then the dreadful guilt of blood
Swept down my soul as winter's flood
    Tosses a riven leaf.

And ever, and still, for thirty years
    That day has been to me
The brand of a curse upon my brow,
And made me all that I am now,
    And all I fear to be.

The penance even of a life
    Hides not a single day;
Oh, shrive me from the weight within,
The guilt of unforgiven sin,
    And let me pass away!

THE BATTLE OF HASTINGS.

On the 27th of September, 1066, after a long and weary waiting on the northern coast of France, William the Norman sailed from St. Valery with a mighty host, to win for himself the sovereignty of England.

For nine months of little ease Harold Godwinson had reigned over Saxons, Danes, and Cambrians, and throughout that period, on both sides of the Channel, great had been the preparations for the struggle raised by the claim of William to the crown. Harold held the throne as one who had been the right hand of the Confessor, who had received the recommendation and nomination of Edward on his death-bed, and who had been chosen as Lord and Father by the assembled chiefs and by the voice of the people. William's claim was based on the facts that Edward's mother had been a Norman princess, that Edward had some years before his death held out to William a hope of succession, and that Harold had been induced, under pressure of detention in Normandy, to swear to become the man of the Norman Duke and to marry one of his daughters, and that he now declined to give up the English lordship, and alleged that he was already married. Neither of these facts would in themselves give William any title to the throne of England, but they served his purpose, gave a colour to his enterprise, and enabled him to hold up his opponent as a perjurer, to be branded with the anathema of the Church.

What the fate of the struggle would have been, if Harold had not been summoned to the north to meet the invasion of Harold Hardrada and Tostig, none can say ; but just before the time when, in answer, as it was thought, to a special appeal to Heaven and to St. Valery, the south wind blew softly, Harold was forced to proceed with an army to York and to fight at Stamford Bridge against the hosts of the Norsemen, leaving the southern coast of his kingdom undefended.

It was on the 25th of September that Hardrada and his men were smitten down, and the storm of Orre was poured fruitlessly on the English force in defence of the Landwaster. The great mass of the Norse army was destroyed ; but many were they who fell on the side of the Saxon monarch, whose arms might, if they had lived, have turned the tide of battle on the low hill of Senlac.

Two days later the south wind blew across the English Channel, and the great fleet of the Normans through the night followed the blazing lantern of the Conqueror towards our coast. On the next day they landed unopposed at Pevensey and took up a strong position at Hastings, from whence they ravaged the surrounding country.

It seems that the news of this invasion was carried to King Harold at York within four days after the disembarkation, and that on the 5th of October he returned to London to take immediate action against William. We may perhaps treat as poetical exaggeration the story that before he left York he was told how the fields glittered with the shining arms of the Normans, how the homes of his people were destroyed by fire, the inhabitants slain with the sword, and the little children left to weep over their slaughtered parents ; but there can be no doubt that by the time he reached the banks of the Thames the tale of the miseries inflicted on the South Saxons by the Norman troops must have been borne to him in all its fulness.

As he marched southward to London, men from all the surrounding counties flocked to the king's standard, and for a week after his arrival he waited there, partly to give time for the men

C

of Wessex to join him, and partly to enable his jealous brothers-in-law, the two northern earls, Morcar and Edwin, to prove that their patriotism was greater than their lust for power. They never came, and it was upon those forces which he could collect from only a portion of his kingdom that the Saxon king was forced to rely in the great day of battle.

During the period of waiting, messages passed between the two opposed leaders. The day and place of battle was fixed, and Harold went to Waltham Abbey, and there, with offerings and prayers, prostrated himself before the holy crucifix ; and there, as we are told, while he prayed the image bowed forward on the nails which held it to the cross, and, as conscious of the coming fate, looked mournfully down on the doomed monarch.

On Thursday, the 12th of October, the journey towards Senlac was begun. It is not a matter of much consequence whether preparations had been previously made for the erection of the long, low rampart of palisading which was destined to protect the front of the English force, or whether the whole of the army followed the king from London. Great general as Harold undoubtedly was, and well acquainted with the post which he meant to defend, we may be sure that every precaution was taken which skill and experience could suggest, and that nothing was left to be collected at the last moment. By the morning of Saturday, October the 14th, if not by the preceding evening, all preparations were completed, and Harold and his men had fortified their camp in a manner which showed how thoroughly he understood the relative powers of the forces.

At the present day we can wander over the grounds where the ruins of Battle Abbey remain. From the terrace which tops the relics of one of the old buildings, we can look down on the low grounds of the valley to the south. The face of the eastern end of the Saxon position shows an abrupt elevation from the field, and towards the west the ground slopes down gradually to reach the level of the land in front of it. In front of the western end is the outlying knoll near which so many fell on both sides, and behind the line to the north was the ravine with its steep sides and marshy bottom, to which the overthrow and death of so many Norman knights gave the name of the Malfosse. Towards the east we can look down into the hollow where the site of the High Altar was discovered, and we can listen to the guide who tells us how the body of Harold was found beneath a clump of gorse near by. The adaptation of the ground for the building of the Abbey, and the alterations and accumulations of eight hundred years, must have considerably altered and in some places raised the surface of the earth. I think it probable that, except at the extreme east, the incline from the south was more gentle than it now appears; but even with this allowance the elevation gradually decreasing towards the west must have given very great strength to the position which the Saxons fortified against the Norman enemy.

A low, strong palisading was planted along the south front, extending almost to the little streamlet which bounded the extreme west. The ascent of the hill, aided by such a defence, must have effectually checked any attack of cavalry on the Saxon line, and have enabled the defenders to rain their darts and axe-strokes at an immense advantage upon all who ventured to test the strength of their position. It was the power of the Norman knights (not to be separated for any length of time from their horses) that was most to be feared; and so long as those horses were kept to the south of the palisade, so long was it impossible for the English army to be worsted in the battle. Behind the line of Harold's chosen troops stood the two standards—one, the Golden Dragon of Wessex, the glorious banner of the West Saxons; the other, Harold's own ensign, the Fighting Man, wondrous to see, en-riched as it was with gilded work and costly stones. The western portion of the Saxon line appears to have been the weakest, but it was protected by men posted on the outlying knoll, who had seen warfare against the Welsh, and who found their natural enemies in the Gaels from over sea. Advancing up the valley with the Bretons and the soldiers from Maine on his left, the Normans in the centre, and the men of Picardy and the French mercenaries on his right, William came within fighting distance of the Saxon post. About nine o'clock in the morning the fight began. At first the archers and the foot soldiers attacked the front. The arrows were met by the wall of shields; the darts and javelins hurled from below were answered with more fatal effect by those cast from above; while those who were able to come within striking distance of the ponderous two-handed axes fell cloven in two by the weight of the blow. Many were slain on both sides; but the advantage was at first with the soldiers of England. Meanwhile, on the left, the Bretons and their companions were met by the defenders of the knoll and the western end of the Saxon line, and were hurled back in confusion. Then it was that an error was made. Harold had expressly ordered that no man should quit his post in the battle; but when the English soldiers saw their foes flying from before them, human nature could not stand the temptation. After them they went; the foreigner was to be slaughtered, and the axes, clubs, swords, and spears had a rich meal of blood. For a time the flight of the Bretons spread a panic through the Norman host; and it was only by superhuman exertions on the part of William and his bravest leaders that at last the flight was checked and order re-established. Then those who had fled turned on their pursuers, surrounded them, and cut most of them to pieces. Again the attack was made, and again it was met. Fiercely and furiously men fought. Gurth and Leofwine, the two brothers of the king, appear, from the Bayeux Tapestry, to have been surrounded and killed, and one of them is believed to have been stricken down by the heavy mace of William of Normandy. During that period of the strife, twice was William himself thrown to the ground, his horse slain under him. On all sides blood was flowing, and axes and swords ringing, while the shouts of the combatants were heard far away from the field of battle. Still Harold the King held his own. Still the twin standards floated in the air; and, if the palisading was broken, there was still behind it the impenetrable shield wall and the stout hearts of the bravest soldiers in Britain.

For nearly six hours the fight had lasted. Could Harold keep his enemy at bay until the setting of the autumn sun he might strengthen himself for the next day, and William's position would be more than dangerous if fresh levies could be brought to bear on his already weakened power. There was no time to be lost ; the victory must be won, if at all, on that day. He passed the word for a feigned attack to be made on the western end of the Saxon line. He accurately estimated the temperament of the men and leaders there posted. By a simulated flight on the part of the foreigners the Saxons were drawn from their entrenchments, and then the returning power of the Norman army surrounded and overwhelmed them, and at last found a footing round the end of the fortification. The Norman horses were seen on the north side of the palisades.

There was now no great natural obstacle in the path of their attack. The slope, probably somewhat rugged and broken, ran up to the banner-stones of Harold, and up this slope the Norman knights charged, while the whole front of the English was engaged with the attack of the main army. But the slope was narrow, and the bristling masses of English warriors had no thought of flight in surrender. Their shields, thick with hostile arrows, still formed a wall, while strong hands hurled back darts or thrust spears through their enemies, and, from above that wall, the tremendous whirl of the long axe clove the helm and broke the sword and strewed the field with horses and riders. Even when, after fearful loss on the part of the Normans, the wall was broken, and the defenders reduced to groups of desperate men, these last sold their lives dearly, and great was the carnage on both sides. Gradually and slowly fighting onward step by step, with their numbers still perishing in front, still increasing from behind, William and his chivalry worked their way towards the standards. There still stood Harold fighting like a monarch for his kingdom, like a hero for his nation. We are told that at this point in the battle William ordered his archers to shoot into the air and so strike the helmets of the Saxons ; and it has been generally supposed that in obedience to this order their arrows were shot high up, so that in falling they might penetrate the

leathern head-covering worn by many of the Saxon soldiers. I
may be wrong, but I have never been able to believe this. An
arrow shot nearly straight up into the air will fall no one knows
where, and a slight current of wind will make a missile so sent
as dangerous to the friends as to the enemies of the archer. I
think that the real order given to them was simply to aim higher
—to shoot, not at the shields, but at the heads of the Saxons.
If we are to judge from the Bayeux Tapestry, the arrow which
struck Harold came, not from above, but on a line with his face,
when his head was slightly thrown backward in the act of striking.
The arrows bristling on his shield have come straight towards
him ; one has passed over the shield, and has struck his right
eye. Grasping desperately at the shaft in the instinctive effort
to withdraw it, the king falls mortally wounded beneath the
standard. A small body of Norman knights—most of whom fell
in the attempt, stricken down by the companions of Harold—
made a desperate rush to the spot. Four of them reached it,
and, with sword and spear, stabbed out the remaining life of the
great Saxon. The Fighting Man was beaten down ; the Golden
Dragon uprooted from its banner-stone, carried away in triumph
to the Conqueror, and the last of the hero band that stood to
defend it smitten to death. Afterwards breath was found in a
few of those chosen warriors, and they were carried away and
lived ; but at the moment when the fight was over around the
standard, not one was supposed to have survived.

The victory was won ; but in the shades of the evening the
light-armed Saxons, who, seeing that all was lost, began to flee,
finding themselves pursued turned on their pursuers and slew
many of them, as, in ignorance of the ground, they fell horse
over man down the steep sides of the Malfosse, until the hollow
was full of writhing forms.

William won the battle and the crown. He may at first have
intended to rule justly ; but he either could not or did not protect
his new subjects from the tyranny and oppression of his followers.
A warlike and independent nation will not willingly yield its
freedom, and the spirit of the Saxons was not likely to submit

without murmur to all the indignities which the Norman conquerors showered down upon them. For years afterwards we
hear of risings to be quelled, of rebels to be punished. Even
where there was apparent obedience, there must have been
inward hatred, and many must have been the conclaves of the
discontented, who, despising their own subservience, eagerly
sought for some means to avenge themselves on their oppressors.
From these meetings the Saxon gleeman would not be absent.
He would remind his hearers of the glories of their fathers, and
stir up the lagging spirit of the faint-hearted, and at times he
would teach them how valiantly the great king strove to defend
his kingdom, and would point to the prophecy of the dying
Confessor, that a day would come when the green tree cut away
from the midst of its trunk should be joined thereto again, and
again put forth leaves and bear fruit in its season, and that then
the woes of England should end. It is to such a song, told to
such a meeting, that I have endeavoured to give words.

NORMAN castles towering round us
    Crush the confiscated land,
All the nation moans in anguish
    Underneath the Norman hand.
Shall we kiss that hand with meekness,
    Bow the knee in humble mood,
In our ears the cries of slaughter,
    In our eyes the mist of blood?

Hear your wives and daughters crying
    For the help ye dare not give;
See your sons and brothers dying,
    And can ye endure to live?

'Twas not thus we met the tyrant
  Upon Senlac's fatal plain,
When the life-blood of our heroes
  Soaked the earth as autumn's rain ;
Still the faithful earth in mourning
  Shows to heaven the crimson stain.

Gather round my harp in silence ;
  List the record of that day,
Till ye hear the crash of armour
  And the shouting in the fray ;
Till the dead in living spirit
  Bid ye battle while ye may.

Tall and stately looked our monarch,
  Harnessed as beseemed a king :
In his hand the axe of battle,
  On his helm the golden ring ;
O'er him waved the ancient Dragon,
  O'er him blazed the Fighting Man,—
As he stood to face his warriors,
  In the forefront of the van.

" Every footstep of the Norman
  Reeks with blood that he has shed ;
In his ears the curse is ringing
  Of the dying and the dead.
Raise to heaven our ancient war-cry,
  Steep your axes deep in gore ;

Strike in freedom's name, and, striking,
   Let the smitten rise no more.
Not for glory or for power
   Are ye gathered to the fight ;
Not for Harold, but for England,
   Strike ; and God defend the right ! "

Then there rose the voice of thousands,
   Like the roaring of the sea,
Shouts of "God and king for ever !"
   Shouts of " Death or liberty ! "
Ceased the tumult, and in silence
   Every head was bowed in prayer,
Trusting honour, life, and country
   Humbly to the Maker's care.

Who shall say the trust is broken,
   Though the Norman gained the field,
And the life-blood of the pleader
   Clotted o'er his riven shield?
Still in memory lives their honour,
   Still in death their souls are free,
Still may leaf and bloom and berry
   Cluster on the stately tree.
Raise again the cry of battle,
   Once again the standard rear,
And in victory and vengeance
   Learn the ending of the prayer.

On they came, the Norman masses,
Gathered in the vale beneath ;
On, in thousands upon thousands,
In the panoply of death,
Like a mighty cloud of tempest
Rolling o'er a blasted heath.
And a shout of proud defiance
Burst in thunder from our van,
And the sunlight flashed in splendour
All around the Fighting Man.

Then, in answer to the thunder
From the tempest cloud below,
Came the lightning rush of arrows
From the archers of the foe ;
And amid the shout of battle,
Like a vast and rolling flood,
Dashed the leaders of the Normans
Where the Saxon heroes stood.

Well they stood in line unyielding,
Dart for dart and stroke for stroke ;
Sweep of axes, thrust of lances,
On the clanging armour broke ;
Sweep of axes, thrust of lances,
Ring of sword on helm and shield,
Call of bugles, shouts and curses,
Madly through the battle pealed.

Foot to foot, no step was yielded,
　　Nought between them save the dead,
Riven shields, and anguish writhing
　　In the blood itself had shed.
Red with gore the lifted axes,
　　Red with gore the spear and sword ;
Blood above them, blood around them,
　　Blood beneath them on the sward.

As the thresher's flail in harvest,
　　Fell the axe of Harold then ;
Under Leofwine, Gurth, and Godric
　　Were the groans of dying men.
And we grasped our axes tighter,
　　And we shouted in our might,
As we saw the foremost waver,
　　As we bore them back in fight.

Proudly, proudly blazed the Dragon,
　　As the war-cry rose again
That so oft before had called him
　　To the banquet of the slain,
When the Raven fell before him,
　　Plumage torn and broken wings,
When the English kites and foxes
　　Battened on the flesh of kings.

Loud and louder rose the clangour,
　　Fast and faster fell the blow ;

Horse and man went down together
  As we charged upon the foe,
As we drove them, fighting, flying,
  Backwards o'er the bloody sod :
There was death and desolation
  Where the English Dragon trod.

But the surges beat upon us,
  As the waves of ocean roar,
In the flood time of the winter,
  Dashed upon a rocky shore.

All unceasing in its power,
  Still that ocean marches on ;
Every wave is stayed and broken—
  Broken ; but its work is done.
Victors still, in lessening numbers,
  Hour on hour we stood at bay ;
Every wave that broke upon us
  Bore some Saxon lives away.

So we fought, and still the sunbeams,
  Slanting from the western sky,
Saw the gold upon our banner,
  Heard untamed our battle-cry.
But we knew our numbers broken,
  As we drew in closer ring
Round the standard of our honour,
  By our hero and our King.

On they came, the Norman horsemen,
    Charging up the sloping hill,
Where the shield wall stood to battle,
    Where the Dragon floated still.
Swifter poured the deadly arrows,
    Like the burst of summer hail,
Piercing through the weakened harness,
    Battered helm, and broken mail.

On they came, the wall was riven,—
    Scattered, desperate of life,
Worn with toil, the Saxon warriors
    Bore them still against the strife.
Earth was cumbered with the dying,
    Where in closing fight they stood,
Dealing death in death, and falling
    'Midst the stream of Norman blood.

Overnumbered by the horsemen,
    Churl and chieftain, side by side,
Pierced by spear-thrust, hacked with broadsword,
    Prince and peasant fought and died.

Still beneath the blazing Dragon
    Harold's axe was whirled around,
And the stricken lay before him,
    Like a rampart on the ground ;
And the boldest of the Normans
    Quailed before that kingly form,

Standing, as a rock of granite,
    In the centre of the storm.

He hath fallen, arrow-smitten ;
    Still he strives to rise in vain.
Dogs, that dared not face him living,
    Stab him, dying, on the plain ;
And as droops a soaring eagle,
    Stricken in its pride of flight,
Fluttering fell the golden Dragon,
    'Midst the shadows of the night.

Long and weary is the darkness—
    Shall we never see the morn ?
Has our glory sunk for ever
    In the bitterness of scorn ?

Cold the hearts that once were valiant,
    Weak the arms that once were strong ;
Saxons crouch before their masters,
    As a dog beneath the thong.

None to raise the wounded Dragon,
    None to staunch the wasting drain ;
Branded with the name of coward,
    Tamely can ye bear the stain ?

No ; I see the dawn is springing,
    Bright and brighter grows the ray.

In your hearts the call is ringing,—
Heed the message while ye may.

Think of all that ye have suffered ;
Raise again the battle brand ;
Let the life-blood of the Norman
Purge the honour of our land.

THE LEGEND OF WILTON LEA.

THERE is a height above the shore,
  And on the height a ruined mound ;
The crumbling stones half lichened o'er,
  Half buried in the ground.
Time and the sea-wind hath defaced
The long-hewn stones, where still is traced
The chevroned work, the patient skill
Of living hearts, of living will.
The broad cliff standeth steep and white,
But just beneath its topmost height
Are two dark caves, like sightless eyes
Aye turned towards the morning skies ;
Or like the orbits of a skull,
All impressionless and dull,
Still suggesting grief and care
In the life that has been there—
Sorrow burdening the birth,
Life that would not leave the earth,
Weary nights and toilsome days
Crushing out the voice of praise,

Till the heavy work was done,
And one goal at least was won.
 All is o'er, the soul hath flown,
 Nothing is left but the silent bone
 Tablet of a parted groan.

There is a narrow dangerous way
Up the tall cliff's white face ; and they
Who have explored those caverns say
There did the sea-bird build her nest,
 There did she rear her young ;
And 'midst the down from off her breast,
And lime, and rough and broken stones,
Were vestiges of human bones,
To which, e'en in their last decay,
 The rust of iron clung.

Unfold the past, roll back the years ;
 Wake from the dust the withered brain,
Once more to live in hopes and fears ;
 Clothe the dry bones with flesh again.

Bid arch and buttress, tower and hall,
 Stand as they did in days of old ;
Fling out the banner from the wall ;
 Let warriors gleam in steel and gold.

They answer not. Nor human breath,
 Nor human eye can pierce the gloom ;

D

No hand can break the seal of death,
  Or roll the door-stone from the tomb.

So let them sleep, and in their stead
  Let Fancy here awhile be crowned,
And weave a legend of the dead,
  A legend of the ruined mound.

Stern and strong the Norman keep
Looked from the height o'er the rolling deep—
Looked from the height o'er the fruitful land,
Reft by the sword from the Saxon's hand.
All that the searching eye could reach,
Forest and meadow and rocky beach,
From the distant hill to the wave of the sea,
Was claimed by the Baron of Wilton Lea.

Fierce in battle and silent in hall,
Stern and cold as his castle wall,
Parting with little and grasping all,
Never a work of mercy done,
Never a word of blessing won,
The baron lived, in heart, alone.

Against the blue of the evening sky the purple clouds
    were rolled ;
'Midst the dark stems of the forest trees flashed the
    long rays of gold.

The lengthening shadows lay in peace on the head
of the yellow corn ;
The lark sent down her voice from the sky, and the
finch from the leaf-clad thorn ;
The sound of slowly homing kine came from the
distant lea,
And tints that fell from the changing clouds made
glory o'er the sea.
All nature smiled in loveliness as to the castle mound
The baron returned from his chase on the moor with
man and hawk and hound.
The day had been long and the quarry strong; o'er
hill and dale they sped,
Until at length the death-shout rang on the top of the
Beacon Head ;
But the heat of the chase had passed away, and weary
their steps and slow,
And the baron's face was worn and stern, and heavy
was his brow.
It may have been that on his soul some darker
memory weighed ;
It may have been that on his head some deeper curse
was laid :
None knew, or cared to ask.   Before his band he rode
alone.
His deeds, perchance, were guessed by all,—his
thoughts were all his own.
And there, before the castle gate, a weary peasant
stood.

There were blood-marks on his hands and feet, and
on his face was blood.

He stood before the baron's path, and raised his hand
on high,

And the stain on the palm bore the deep dark hue of
blood that hath long been dry.

"Thine are the fruits in the barns," he said, "and the
beasts on the lea and the moor.

From all that God hath sent to thee deal kindly with
the poor.

I have come from far away, and have not where to
lay my head ;

I ask but a place wherein to rest, and the gift of a
morsel of bread."

The baron gazed on the hand upraised, and the
haggard, blood-stained face,

He had smitten the speaker to the ground but for
God's saving grace.

And cold and stern the answer came, "Get shelter
where ye will ;

Feed on the berries from the bush, find water in the rill."

"Now, nay, great chief," the stranger said, "but hear
me when I pray ;

No blessings light upon the roof when the poor is
driven away."

The wrath, half checked before, blazed forth. "Have,
then, thy prayer," he said ;

"Thy food the garbage of the soil, the dungeon stone
thy bed."

A word, a sign ; the Norman train around the suppliant close.
They hale him through the castle gates with jeers and
scathing blows,
They drag him where the caverned cell lies deep in
the white cliff's side,
Where two small chinks let in the light that comes
o'er the eastern tide —
Two feeble glimmering rays of light ; a rank and loath-
some den,
Foul with the moanings of despair and the deaths of
starving men.
And there they cast the fainting form, and, at their
lord's command,
Around the victim's waist they clenched the ponderous
iron band
Chained to a beam. For food they gave a crust all
fouled with gore,
And bade him drink of the drops that fell from the
roof on the putrid floor.

The baron returned to the banquet hall. The wine
was bright and red,
But still he saw in the wassail-cup the blood that he
had shed.
Below the board the menials sate, and the song was
loud and high,
But still through the shouts the baron heard the moans
of agony.

He turned to his couch. No peace was his ; the
    victims he had slain
Gathered around his restless sleep, and showed their
    wounds again ;
And the cry of woes his hand had wrought rang
    through the fevered brain.
Out driven in his dream at last, he wandered in a wood
Where corpses mingled with the trees and water
    changed to blood.
And still the cry of doom rang forth, behind him and
    around,
And, as he ran, dead hands stretched forth and clutched
    him to the ground.
In vain, with piteous gaze, he sought to find some
    saving goal ;
No voice in heaven or earth to plead for mercy on his
    soul.
At last, at last, through the midnight drear, one feeble
    ray of light,
And a low soft call that seemed to break the horrors
    of the night.
In desperate hope he struggled on, yet still behind
    him came
The shade of death, the sea of blood, the vengeance,
    and the flame.
O'er broken ground, through tearing thorn, still must
    he press the race,
And die, if he may win in death a hallowed resting-
    place.

And the voice grew sweet, and the beacon bright ; but
    when the strife was o'er,
A broken man the baron fell beside the opened
    door.

And One came forth and raised him up, and bare him
    in His hand,
And spake in words of peace, and there was silence
    in the land ;
And ministered with gentle touch, all fainting as he
    lay,
And cooled and healed his wounded limbs, and
    washed the stains away.
But then, as sense and thought returned, before the
    baron's eye
Uprose the hand with the stain on the palm of blood
    that hath long been dry.
The baron gazed on the hand upraised, he gazed on
    the blood-stained face,
And a cry burst forth from his inmost soul as he knelt
    at the feet of Grace,
And once again he heard that voice which he had
    scorned before,
" Behold, thy sins are all forgiven ; depart and sin no
    more."
He woke, and started from his bed. The dawn was
    in its birth,
And the soft sounds of coming day went upward from
    the earth.

With hasty foot and trembling frame he trod the
winding stair,
He turned the prison door, but lo! no prisoner was
there.
Useless the chain hung from the beam, empty the
iron band,
And fair the cave in the morning light as blessed by
an angel's hand ;
And carved upon the hallowed wall, in gentle beauty
smiled
A symbol of redeeming love—the Mother and the
Child.

No more as Baron of the Lea—within that sacred
cell
For many a year the hermit prayed, as ancient legends
tell.
The iron ring of massive weight that once his Saviour
bore,
Chained to the beam, around his waist in penitence
he wore ;
His wealth, his lands to holy hands and charity
resigned.
God grant that he hath found His grace, and that we
too may find.

THE HERO'S WELL.

HIGH on the rock where Gibeon stands alone,
The sentinel of Zion, Judas sate.
Far to the west, in azure and in gold,
The ocean rose to meet the setting sun.
But nearer than the sea there lay the shore ;
And nearer than the shore there stood the hills ;
And 'midst the hills, like snakes, the valleys crept,
E'en from the margin of the distant plain
Up to the very bastions of God ;
And 'midst them all there lay the Syrian host
In might and numbers, like a leprous curse
Blighting the hope and promise of the land.

It well may be that, in the books of heaven,
The wailing of an infant in its pain
Is marked and chronicled by angels' hands ;
But the full anguish of a nation's wrong
Finds itself wings, and, bursting from the earth,
Stamps its own record on the living page.

From Galilee the cry of blood arose—
The blood of man, of woman, and of child ;
The blood of those who bowed them to the stroke,
And only called on Heaven ; blood without stint ;—
Until the earth, sealing her patient breast,
Held the dark stain up to the frowning sky.

It seemed as though no eye beheld the slain,
And the death-cry that gasped its way to heaven
Found e'en the home of God untenanted,
And earth and sky were desolate.   How hard
To learn that vengeance cometh from the Lord ;
To wait, and, as it seems, to wait in vain ;
To bear in hope ; to linger on in hope ;
To die unsatisfied, nor hear afar
The rushing murmur of His chariot-wheels !
" Hath He indeed forgotten to be true,
And cast us off for ever ?   Can it be
That we have loved and trusted Him for nought ?
Will He not come ?   How long, O Lord, how long ? "

At last uprose the chieftain of the hills,
Judas the Maccabee, and, strong in faith,
Strong in the memory of his victories,
Girt on the sword won in the flush of war,
Upraised his standard for a rallying point,
And stood between the living and the dead.

But unto him came a bare thousand men,
While two and twenty thousand hostile swords
Chafed in their scabbards, and the plunging hoofs
Of twice a thousand horses tore the ground,
For want of corpses to be trampled on.

But Judas and his men were on the hills,
And came to Gibeon.   Then, because he knew
That many hearts were troubled with affright,
And doubts were in their councils, for a space
The chief withdrew him from the gloomy camp,
And climbed the mountain, seeking on its height
Companionship with Heaven and his thoughts.

And there he sate until the sun went down,
Discerning many memories in his heart,
But seeing all the future like a night.
He knew the power of his enemies ;
He knew the weakness of his followers.
Retreat or battle : and if battle, death ;
And if retreat, dishonour.   Every thought
Fell overburdened with a double weight ;
And the old spirit that in by-gone days
Had borne him past obstruction, till his foes
Fled from before his name, was his no more.

And there he sate until the vanquished sun,
Fighting the darkness even in its death,
Buried its rays beneath the western sea.

Then, as its power faded from the earth,
And sea and sky joined in the requiem,
Judas arose, one hand upon his spear,
The other on the rock, and looked around,
And saw and trusted to the love of God.
And a great peace came o'er him, and he knelt,
Bowing his head down even to the dust,
And worshipped, and returned unto the camp.

He called his followers; and they came around,
Lingering and sad. He marked the downcast eye,
The lip indented, and the sinewy hand
Firm clenched against itself, as if in hate
Of the weak soul that kept it from the fight.
They came around. The torches in the night
Cast not more fitful change of light and shade
O'er helmet, shield, and spear, o'er face and limb,
Than in their hearts the momentary flash
Of bravery, not firm enough to dare,
Rose up and died away again, and left
The gloom of fear that struggled to be brave.

And so they stood in silence as he spake :
" The enemies are many ; we are few.
But when did the Almighty first begin
To take account or number of His foes ?
When did He send an ambassage of peace,
Or render tribute to His conquerors ?
Have we not heard how, in the days of old,

When Israel was weak and trodden down,
The Lord arose, and, with an arm of might,
With hailstones cast from heaven, with angels' hands,
With the broad flashes of His thunderstorm,
The kings and captains of the earth were slain,
And Jacob dwelt in safety?   And whene'er
His cause was trusted to the swords of men,
Those swords were swayed by more than human might,
And single warriors told of thousands slain.
Who raised up Samson, Gideon, and Saul?
Who gave the Philistine to David's sling,
And blessed us with an everlasting name?
Is the Lord's eye less keen, weaker His arm,
Than in those days of great deliverance?"
He paused, and as he paused he looked around;
Yet answer came there none, except a sigh
And a slow shaking of the downcast head,
And then at last a low and murmured sound,
"Let us return.   To fight is but to die."

He swept his hand a moment o'er his face,
As blotting out remembrance of the past.
And when he spake, his voice was low and clear,
But hollow as the dropping of a knell.

"Ye may be right.   But I am God's alone.
I dare not hesitate, and unto death
Must remain constant where the heart is bound.
I will not bid you follow; but I go.

And if I go unaided, 'tis from Him ;
And if I die alone, I do but die
A sacrifice of peace.   Grant me but this :
Redeem my body.   Lay it in the tomb
Wherein my fathers sleep, and say of me
I could not live with Israel in chains ;
And bless me in my memory.   Fare ye well."

He laid his own on Eleazar's hand,
The nearest and the bravest of his friends,
Pressed it, and uttered once again, " Farewell."
And, looking with an eye that seemed to look
Out of the world into eternity,
Eye into eye and through it, blessed them all,
And would have turned.   But ere the words were
      sped,
A murmur, like the rushing of a wind,
And then a long-drawn sob, and then a cry,
Burst from the little band in unison :
"We all are thine.   Do with us as thou wilt."
And spears and swords flashed upwards, and the men
Close gathered round with short and broken words,
And earnest eyes filled with unwonted tears.
And Eleazar, bending o'er the hand
Still resting on his own, in trembling voice
Spake in the name of all: " Thy God is ours ;
Where thou art we are.   Even unto death
We are but one.   Forgive us."   And the cry
Ran through the band, " Father, forgive thy sons ! "

A moment—and a cloud o'erdimmed the eye,
The dark plume quivered, and the labouring breath
Rose like the surges of a troubled sea,
As, head and face thrown upward to the sky,
And lips drawn firm, he stemmed the tide of heart
Rising within him.   Then he spake again.

" I was but now like to the child that lay
Within the chamber of the Shunamite,
And your then love was as the prophet's staff
That gave no life.   Now, hand is joined to hand,
And heart to heart, and living love to life.
Ye have done well, and memory is with God ;
And the proud history of faithfulness
Shall blazon in the annals of the land ;
That every name shall be in coming times
A cloud of fire to lead God's champions on.
Farewell until to-morrow.   Rest and pray."

The ring of shield and spear within the camp
Awoke the dawn, and ere the sun arose
The little army gathered in array.
No doubts were there ; but earnest, living zeal,
Girding the soul to battle, till it longed
To prove itself the birthright of the Lord.

Then the low sounds that mounted to the sky
Taught the young light the hallowed words of prayer—
" Father and Chief, the day is in Thine hands ;

Our lives are Thine—Thine only.   Take or spare,
Even as seemeth best.   For, taking them,
Thine own are only taken to Thyself;
But spare them, if Thou wilt, for the dear sake
Of those we fight for.   Yet Thy will be done."
Then, as the words uprose, the march began,
And Judas passed before them on the way.

Onward they went until the vale was gained
Where lay the Syrian army, all outspread,
Like a huge dragon, cumbering the ground.
A narrow pass was at the valley's head ;
On either side the dark and barren rocks
Stood scowling at the chasm, as in hate
That they, despite themselves, were thrust aside
To make a pathway for the will of God.

They entered in, and, with extended front,
Filling the passage even to the hills,
Halted in expectation of the foe ;
But scarce their sheen had glittered down the vale,
When in the hostile camp a trumpet blast
Made note of preparation.   To and fro
The sounds of arms and cries were tossed about,
Like echoes from a cave, and the vast bounds
Seethed out their soldiers, till the line grew strong,
And stars of light glittered throughout the plain,
Shot from the bright caparison of war.

Then the loud signal of advance was made,
And forward rushed the army, like a wave
With tossing crests, towards the narrow pass.
Onward they came until the space between
Had dwindled to a furlong. Then they stayed;
And for a while the men on either side
Stood sternly and in silence—in a calm
Too dead to last. The very breath was drawn
In troubled snatches, and the hands were clenched
Until the spear-points trembled with a pulse.

Then the deep still was broken as a glass,
Sounded the charge, and forward, with a shout,
The rushing armies met in mid career.
Thousands were launched at hundreds; but the last,
Flanked by the rocks, gave not an inch of ground,
But bore them up as thousands. Every man
Bore death before him, life within his heart.
On pressed the Syrians, as a band of wolves
Panting for blood, till dying in their own;
Or like the waves upon a tideless sea,
That beat and beat for ever on the strand,
But gain no vantage. Then the Maccabee,
Noting the war with ever-watchful eye,
Bade blow the trumpet with a mightier blast;
And, as a rock rolls down upon the plain,
The Jewish warriors dashed upon the foe,
When the attack was waning. Then the play
Of sword-blades flashing in the morning sun,

E

Scattering the life-drops as they rose and fell,
Grew thick and fast ; and shouts, and dying groans,
And the wild clang of steel rose o'er the hills,
And bore the tale of death to distant towns.

A little while—the onward course was stayed ;
A little while—the din of answering blows ;
A little while—the shout that echoed shout :
But as the sword of Judas rose to smite,
Nor wearied of its smiting, every blow
Supplied a gap for "Onwards ;" and the cry
Of "Onwards !" followed with the curse of death.
The leading ensigns wavered, rose, and sank ;
And, backward borne, yet fighting to the last,
The choicest warriors of Syria's host
Fell in their blood, and rank and order lost—
All was confusion until all was flight.
And mingled spears, and swords, and helms, and shields,
And broken staves, and corpses strewed the ground.

In vain the leaders sought to stem the rout,
To wage encounter with the rushing tide.
Onward it swept, and bore them on its crest ;
And onward, like an eagle in its flight,
Smiting and sparing not, the victor host
Swept after, in the vengeance of the Lord.

And so the sword of slaughter dashed along,
Until the day was weary of its dead,

And the worn victors kept nor rank nor place,
And loitered in the slaying.   Then they paused
Hard by the well that is in Beeroth.

But then, as ye have seen a little cloud
Gathering the vapour even as it rolled
Until it darkened all the firmament,
So, one by one, the straggling Syrians came,
Men who escaped and let the fight go by,
Unto one head, and, gathering arms and force,
Outnumbering the victors, followed them,
And came upon them in their weariness.

The battle rose again ; but worn and faint,
And scattered in the field, the patriot band
Fought, slaying to be slain.   The tired arm
Scarce raised the shield, and weak and short the blow.

Walled round with foes, but fighting like a god,
Bleeding but killing, bearing death in death,
Judas stood fast o'er Eleazar's corpse,
Until the stream that flowed from many wounds
Wavered the hand, and, as the sight swam round,
Seeking a foe in vacancy, he sank ;
And then a shout arose.   The fight was won.

They gathered round, and, as they stood and gazed,
The eyelids opened, and with gasping lips

He groaned for water.   Even Syrian hearts
Bent at the sound.   They filled a vacant helm
With water from the well.   He drank and died.

Two thousand years and more have come and gone,
And many a foreign host hath borne its arms
O'er the fair land that Judas died to save.
Scattered and peeled, as aliens in the world,
In other climes the tribes of Jewry roam ;
And the appointed garden of the Lord
Mourns for His people, but it mourns in vain.
Yet to this day, using unwitting words,
The Arab guide will bid the traveller stop
And mark the ruin of the Hero's Well.

THE FELON'S RACE.

THE summer sun is on the earth,
The corn is joying in its birth,
And you might think the sleeping sea
Dreamt of its own immensity,
And the light wavelets in their flow
Were but its breathings soft and low.
There is joy in the land, there is joy in the hall,
Welcome and plenty for one and all ;
And Stainby's gates are opened wide
To greet the bridegroom and the bride,
And shouts and laughter come over the lea,
And the gush of bells in their jubilee—
Bells that bear in every tone
Blessings on those who now are one.

They are seen from the wall, a goodly throng.
Cease for a moment the feast and the song ;
Up from the tables and round to the gate,—
When the master is coming the flagon can wait.

Nearer they came, till all might tell
The name of every rider well.
And foremost of the bright array
Ralph of the Keep on his gallant bay,
And gently resting on his side
Is the tender hand of the new-made bride.
And he gathers it up within his own,
Flesh of his flesh, bone of his bone,
And turns to whisper in her ear
Words of blessing, words of cheer,
Words that none besides may hear,
Words that find their sole replies
In gentle touch and loving eyes.

The shouts are echoing o'er the tide
As up the narrow causeway ride
    The leaders of the band.
Yet, ere is reached the clamorous crowd,
Sudden a ring sounds sharp and loud.
From yon low bush a little cloud
    Uprises like a hand.
With one short gasp, one cry of pain,
One fevered tossing of the mane,
    One quick convulsive bound,
Ere yet the life-blood finds its way
Through to the light, the gallant bay
    Falls headlong to the ground.

For one brief moment all was still.
It passed, and o'er the startled hill

Shouting, and cry, and dint of steed
Urged onward to the utmost speed,
　And curses loud and high,
And long-drawn sobs, and shrieks for aid,
And pistol shot and clang of blade
　Rang upward to the sky.

As lion at the scent of foes,
Quick from the dust Ralph Stainby rose,
Unhurt, but crimsoned with the gore
Of the slain horse, and, rising, bore,
Safe held within his sheltering arm,
All pale and breathless with alarm,
His latest gift.　His flashing eye
One moment sought his enemy ;
Marked how his kinsmen scoured the heath
Whence flew the messenger of death ;
Saw, like a quarry from the hounds,
With desperate race and frantic bounds,
O'er gorse and ditch and broken hedge,
Striving to gain the mountain's edge,
Only one man.　A pitying light
Passed o'er his visage at the sight.
He turned, his darling's fears to quell,
And learn and show that all was well.
And then, as quickly gathered round,
Hiding the blood-encumbered ground,
Servant and stranger, kin and friend,
Their care to speak, their aid to lend,

With one long glance in sorrow cast
On that poor friend whose love had passed,
'Midst gratulations long and deep,
Slowly they moved towards the keep.

On to the cliff, in headlong strife,
    Fleet as the footsteps of the wind,—
On to the cliff, the prize is life,
    The roar of blood is close behind,—

On to the cliff, with pant and strain,
    With bleeding limbs and garments torn,
The only chance of life to gain,
    O'er heath and brake and tangled thorn,

He dashes on, a desperate man,
    To where the mighty steeps descend.
The speed with which that race began
    Can scarce continue to the end.

Behind him press the bitter foe,
    Their bullets hurtle in the air,
And gleaming bright are swords that know
    To smite, but know not how to spare.

On to the cliff!   The goal is nigh,
    It needeth but one struggle more ;
Near and more near, the venger's cry
    Is fiercer than a tiger's roar.

Down !   No, 'twas but a moment's thrill
That stayed the runner's course.
Onwards he dashes up the hill,
Straining for life his dying force.

The cliff is won, pursuit is o'er.
There is a passage from the head,
Broken and rough, towards the shore,
But few there be that dare to tread.

Downward he goes.   The cliff is high.
O God, it is a fearful sight !
Sure must the foot be, clear his eye
Who tries that path and treads aright.

Downward the foemen cast their eyes,
As gathered on the height they stand,
And the deep curse of balked surprise
Sounds sternly 'mid the wondering band.

Light as the sea-bird on the wing,
Fresh from its rest at dawn of day,
With step and spring, with grasp and swing
Adown the cliff he wins his way.

A flash of light, a ringing shot,
The echo of a stifled groan,
A white despairing face, a blot
Of crimson on the virgin stone,

A clutching of the feeble hand,
  A yielding of the palsied knee,
A low dead fall upon the strand,
  And—a great silence o'er the sea.

The chase was o'er.   Long time hath sped,
And children long since born are dead
Beneath the weight of years.   Decay
Hath worn the crumbling cliffs away,
Yet to the broken margin still,
From yon black stone far down the hill,
A path the husbandmen can trace,
And call the track the Felon's Race.

THE LAST OF THE FAIRIES.

A LOW sad wail at Christmas-tide.   The morning sun
   is bright,
And the rime, unthawed upon the ground, is sparkling
   in the light.
No breath of wind to stir the leaves that loved the
   wind so well;
That loved its kisses till they died what time the
   autumn fell.
The old old time is dying, and the leaves are dead
   and sere;
But a promise lies in the dawning day and the birth
   of the coming year.
The squirrel sleeps in its mossy nest, in spring to
   wake again;
There's a flutter of life in the tiny heart of the
   autumn-buried grain,
And the frozen brook shall melt in the sun, and swell
   with the early rain.

The heavens above are singing, "God's arms are
　　opened wide,"
And on earth the bells are ringing, "Welcome to
　　Christmas-tide."
Yet, from yon withered bracken tuft, there comes a
　　low sad cry,
As of one who hath no joy to live, yet dares not hope
　　to die.
As the wintry wind at midnight through the boughs of
　　a blasted tree,
The last of all the fairy race moaned in her misery.

"All, all alone in a world of life !　For me no sister's
　　hand ;
I can but trace in blighted rings the steps of the fairy
　　band.
The glories of the summer night are lost in the
　　winter day,
And the very echoes of our songs have long since
　　died away.
New summer nights will not restore the voices of the
　　dead ;
New blades will grow untrodden where their feet were
　　wont to tread.
Without a joy, without a hope ; a shadow and a
　　sigh ;
The gift of life is broken now, and cancelled when I
　　die,

I've heard that with the race of man life lies not in
the breath;
There's a wondrous joy above the sky after an earthly
death.
It may be so—I do not know,—but unto us is given
The power below to feel our woe, without a hope of
heaven."

Then brighter grew the morning sun, and brighter
shone the rime,
And clearer rang the distant bells, "Welcome to
Christmas time.
Goodwill and living love to all. God's arms are
opened wide."
"Welcome," the glorious heavens sang. "Welcome,"
the earth replied.

"False earth, false sky," the fairy said, "what
welcome can there be?
What welcome to the withered leaves? What welcome
unto me?"
Again she moaned, "The coming year cannot revive
the past;
Time can but bring me misery, and pain and death
at last."

Then, in the glow of the warming sun, the frost gems
thawed away,
And countless drops of glittering dew shone in the
light of day,

And under their sheen lay the emerald green of the
    soft and glossy sward,
And every drop and every blade sang, " Glory to the
    Lord ! "
Then the sweet bells ceased, but from the church
    there came the voice of song ;
Gently it stole from the distant porch, and swelled as
    it rolled along ;
And to the open sky uprose that wondrous note of
    praise,
And the dew passed upward with it, in the path of the
    warming rays.
Then a great peace reigned on all the earth, and the
    fairy turned on the sod,
And hid herself from the light, in fear of the accents
    of her God.

She listened : all was silent.   She looked, but all was
    still,
From the forest glade in the vale below to the top of
    the far-off hill ;
And the peace that was around her enwrapped her as
    she lay,
Till in the silent depth of sleep her sorrow died away.

And, in her dream, she saw the leaves, all bare and
    brown and dead,
Lie blown and scattered by the wind, or where they
    had been shed ;
But each in its allotted place, and not as chance had led.

For angels marked the falling seed, and smoothed the
    bed in love,
And gently placed the withering leaves around it and
    above.
The leaves that had cherished the infant seed, as they
    grew on the parent stem,
Still watched in death o'er the tender germ, and God
    watched over them.
And all the long long winter their mould lay close
    and warm,
And shielded it from frost and snow, and shielded from
    the storm ;
Till as the year grew soft and clear uprose the first-
    born shoots ;
And then still closer in decay they gathered round
    the roots,
And mingled with the rising sap, and in new leaf and
    flower
Joyed as of old in the throb of life, and blessed the
    breeze and shower.
And, as through every vein the sap in living impulse
    poured,
The dead leaves, sprung again to life, sang, " Glory to
    the Lord ! "

And then at last there came a voice, " God loveth
    not in vain,
And love sent down, or stays on earth, or turns to
    God again :

And life is love, and God is love—the breath of His
    own word ;
Therefore all living, loving things cry, 'Glory to the
    Lord !'
In love He giveth life, with life the power to love is
    given,
And God's own essence, love, returns to live in God
    in heaven."

Perchance it was the lesson that the dream and voice
    had taught ;
Perchance some angel blessed her with the peace that
    passeth thought ;—
I do not know, and may not say : but when at last
    she woke,
Her heart went forth to join the words that all around
    her spoke.

"Not all alone—not all alone.   Where'er the wind
    can blow,
Be mine to feel another's joy, to soothe another's woe ;
In kindly thoughts, and kindly words, to render God
    His own ;
And in the unison of love to be no more alone ;
And when the hand of death my life shall from the
    earth dissever,
That life shall fade in love, and love shall be with
    God for ever."

THE LEGEND OF HAWKSTONE CASTLE.

I.

IT was in the days of the fairies, in the days so long
    ago,
When the glades of the woods were filled at night with
    music weird and low,
When the moonlight smiled as tiny forms across the
    beams would pass,
And daylight showed the rings their steps had left
    upon the grass.

II.

The Lord of Hawkstone and his men forth to the
    chase had gone,
And by the wood, with babe on arm, his lady sat
    alone,—
Her firstborn babe, her own, that laid so dear against
    her breast.
The setting sun showed clear and broad low down
    upon the west :

F

The lady saw the golden light that tinged the castle
wall,
And where on mound and winding stream the
lengthening shadows fall;
And o'er and round her, as she sat amidst the clustering trees,
Came the twittering of the nesting birds, the droning
of the bees.
The eye scarce saw, the ear scarce heard; but scene
and music stole
Like a gentle dream of gladness o'er the beating of
the soul.
And slowly from her lips as dropped some now-for-
gotten lay,
A deep sleep on that lady came at closing of the day.

III.

The latest gleams of sunlight had left the mountain
head;
One by one the stars looked down to see if the day
had fled,
And, peering through the gathering night, called on
the moon to rise,
And decked themselves in robes of light to meet her
in the skies.
Then through the wood the fairy horn, with strange
and mystic swell,
Awoke the fays that slumbering lay in flow'ret, fern,
and dell;

And o'er the green, around the queen, to pay the
    homage due,
Skimming along with shout and song the little army
    flew ;
And in and out, with song and shout, passed on the
    elfin band,
And the moonbeams glance on flight or dance as
    guides the leader's wand ; .
Through dell and glade, through light and shade,
    encircling round and round,
Till they came where that lady fair lay sleeping on
    the ground.

IV.

Obedient to the queen's command,
A moment paused the rushing band ;
Then, at a sign, arrayed the ring
In silence deep, with folded wing,
Till softly rose in measured chime
The chanting of the magic rhyme.

V.

" Through the woods and on the hill,
    In the shadowland of night,
Where the darkness croucheth still ;
    Where the moon is shining bright ;
Where the silver stars can peep,
    Looking down with liquid ray ;

Where the gentle flowers sleep,
  Waiting for the coming day,—
There at night we freely roam,
For the woodland is our home.

" Wheresoever falls the dew,
  All that meet us on the way
Learn to pay the ransom true ;
  None may dare to disobey.
Since the fairy's reign began
  On the stream and on the wold,
Ours it is to bless or ban,
  Ours to loose and ours to hold.
When the night has called the hour,
All are in the fairies' power.

" While the ring our footsteps make
  Circled round the place of rest,
Lo, the sleeping babe we take
  Gently from its mother's breast,
Seal the sleep upon her eyes,
  Close the ear and numb the sense,
Till secure we hold the prize
  Gathered in its innocence:
Fairies, now the deed is done ;
She has lost, and we have won."

VI.

Gently they moved, in order meet,
To the cadence low and sweet,
Round the sleepers and the queen,
Clad in robes of wondrous sheen.
While the measure rose and fell,
You might have seen them passing well
    In ring of glittering light;
But as the latest accents died
In echoes at the forest side,
There came the rush as of a blast,
And queen and band and infant passed
    Away from mortal sight.

VII.

The wondering servants waited long; at last, in doubt
    and fear,
Through the deep gloom of night they sought their
    lady far and near.
They sought her in the castle ground, beside the
    winding stream;
They saw the shadow of the bat, they heard the
    night bird scream.
Among the gorse, and o'er the mound, and through
    the spreading plain,
With deepening fears they called and looked, but
    called and looked in vain,

Until they found her, all alone, wrapt in her slumber
still,
Beneath the deep-branched trees upon the rising of
the hill.

VIII.

Time past. The seekers for the child returned, their
quest not won :
With man and hound they scoured the ground, but
traces found they none ;
And village crones might guess and talk, none knew
and none might say
Or how or where the infant heir of Hawkstone passed
away.

IX.

The lady lay within her bower, hard beaten by the
blow,
Her soul bent down to earth beneath the crushing
weight of woe.
From morn to night she moaned, and wept from night
to morn again,
Nor night nor morning brought relief from the deep-
driven pain.
In vain the sorrowing baron strove to soothe with
loving care
The dark deep wound of misery encankered by
despair.

At times she slept, but in her sleep no kindly light
　　was given ;
No rest could bless with peace a life from which all
　　joy was riven.
She lived to die. At last, at last, when death seemed
　　drawing near,
And sleep forerunning death had brought strange
　　voices to her ear,
Nor form, nor certain sound was there. She dreamt,
　　and that was all,
But on her in the dream a hope from heaven seemed
　　to fall ;
Like dew upon the tender grass, its gentle influence
　　spread,
Till it gathered the strength of the voice that raised
　　the living from the dead.
She woke, she rose, she called for food. So bright
　　and strange her eye,
Her maidens thought the fire of life had risen but to
　　die.
She spake—a power was in her speech ; and silently,
　　in dread,
The listeners heard her utterance as a message from
　　the dead.
Few were her words. Her accents fell in clear and
　　ordered tone,—
'Twas hers that night to seek the wood untended and
　　alone.

X.

The night has come, and o'er the stream the lady held
    her way,
To where, upon the rising hill, the silent moonbeams
    lay.
They watched her from the castle wall all in the clear
    moonlight,
Until, beneath the branching trees, she faded from
    the sight.

XI.

Clad in robes of wondrous sheen
Around the beauty of the queen,
Elfin knight and lady fay,
Heralds and minstrels in fair array,
Brightest and best of the fairy band,
Ranged in marshalled order stand.

XII.

"Sound the blast.   Let the word go forth,
East and west, and south and north,
Whoso hath suffered from fairy's spite
Let him come and challenge the act to-night.
The court has met to hear the cause
According to the fairy laws,
Long since by masters wise ordained,
That the right be held and the wrong restrained,

And justice rendered clear."
Three times the trumpet blast was heard,
And thrice the heralds raised the word,
  "Let all who will appear."

XIII.

Many a year has passed and gone
Since last before the fairy throne
    The challenge answer found.
Yet still on the appointed night
Their lady held the ancient rite,
    And bade the trumpets sound.

XIV.

To-night they sound, but who shall dare,
When called, alone to venture there?
Though he who wins may bear away,
Who loses there for aye must stay,
And forfeit all his human life
In punishment for bootless strife.

XV.

The trumpets ceased.   Their closing sound
Passed through the echoes all around
    In softly thrilling fall.
A human foot is on the sod,
A human form beneath the trees,

A human voice upon the breeze
Speaks boldly : " In the name of God,
   I answer to the call.
From the bed of death and pain
I come to claim my own again.
    God gave to me a child
Fair as the heaven above. But you,
Seeking to make the gift untrue,
Fouling the love in mercy sent
Down from the blessèd firmament,
Wrought your dark magic as he lay,
And stole the sleeping babe away.
In this, your Court of Right, I claim
My own, in His the Holiest name,
    Holy and undefiled."

XVI.

" The child has been bathed in the midnight dew ;
His brow has been marked by the mystic yew ;
He has slept on the moss to the lullaby
Of the night-winds' whirl and the owlets' cry,
Wrapped in the skin of the speckled snake,
Where the glow-worms wind beneath the brake.
Every rite has been duly done
To win him and keep him and make him our own.
In the fairy land, in the hour of night,
We found him asleep 'neath the moonbeams bright,
And the spell we wrought as we bore him away
Will bind his soul to the judgment day."

XVII.

Stately and firm the lady stood,
Though for a space the coward blood
Had fled towards the troubled heart
    And left her face so pale.
Her lips were slightly drawn apart,
And through them came the quickened breath
As when a sleeper laboureth
    To cry without avail.

XVIII.

Words to the tongue, blood to the cheek
Returned.   She raised her head to speak,
And, though the soul was all in flame,
Slow and clear the accents came.
"Your rites can never move," she said,
"The blessing that on him was laid,
What time before the sacred shrine
His brow was marked with the hallowed sign,
    His sins all washed away.
My child, my own, to me was given;
My love is sanctified by Heaven,
    Strong as the light of day.
And in that strength of love I came
To claim my child, and bear him home,
    To dare the strength ye own.

Let elfin knight take spell and brand,
As here, all weaponless, I stand,
   A woman, and alone.
I claim the trial of the fight,
And Heaven shall prove which has the right,
   And thus my love be shown."

She spake, and angry brows were seen,
   And angry murmurs rose,
As, gathering round their startled queen,
   The hurried council close.

XIX.

Many a year had come and gone
Since last before the fairy throne
   Such challenge had been given ;
And scarce could mortal tongue have power
To brave them in the midnight hour,
   Save by the will of Heaven.
The court may not the claim deny,
Nor champion from the conflict fly,
And thus, at last, with troubled eye,
Slowly the monarch made reply :
   " Be it as thou hast said.
But if thy boasted powers fail,
If hand or tongue or spirit quail,
If spell or spear or brand prevail,
   Thy blood be on thy head.

Bring in the prize." By hands unseen
Unharmed upon the sward of green
 The sleeping babe was laid.
One look of love the mother sent,
One sob of love her bosom rent ;
 She bowed the head and prayed.

XX.

As carved in marble stood she there,
And, save by look and sob and prayer,
 Nor motion made nor sign ;
With folded arms and bended head,
Waiting the onslaught dark and dread,
 In trust on power Divine.

XXI.

The fairy train hath passed. A gloom
Like that which by the prophet's doom
 O'er Egypt's land was spread,
Like a thick mantle gathered slow ;
And then came shrieks and screams of woe,
And wild winds rushing to and fro,
And phantom lights of sickly glow,
 And visions of the dead.

Around they drew, but none might dare
To pierce the atmosphere of prayer.
 In vain ; nor sound nor sight

Might check the words that rose on high,
Nor draw one glance, nor cause one cry
    Of anguish or affright.

Baffled they fled, and silence fell
On the thick wood and startled dell
Awhile ; and then the champion came,
Girt in a panoply of flame,
    His charger red with blood.
Rushing down with headlong force,
Swift as the storm-fiend in his course,
    To where the lady stood,
Onward he came.   A fruitless race ;
Still the lady held her place.
Though thick and fast his falchion swept
Ever her guard an angel kept,
    And turned the blows aside.
And love a sanctuary made,
Broke down the terror of his blade,
    And all his power defied.

XXII.

So went the fight, till, unsubdued,
By faith, by prayer, by love endued,
    She seized his lifted hand.
Vainly to loose that clasp he strove,
The mighty power of mother's love
    Tore down the useless brand.

Trembling he stands before her now ;
She signs the cross upon his brow,
   The cross upon his breast.
And as he falls before her feet,
She hears in accents low and sweet,
   " Lo, I have given thee rest."

XXIII.

Then through the forest's echoes broke
   One long, low sob of joy,
As underneath the branching oak
   She knelt to raise her boy.

THE LIFEBOAT.

THE hollow voice of Winter
   Came moaning to the land ;
With deepening frown, as the sun went down,
   She scowled upon the strand.
Her blast came o'er the waters
   In fitful gusts, and strong,
As she howled to the waves of coming death,
   And hurried them along.
The startled billows heard her,
   And tossed their crests on high ;
And, rushing madly to the shore,
   They shouted in reply.
The white cliffs heard the summons,
   As onward still it flew ;
And rock and cavern, echoing loud,
   Screamed forth the curse anew.
As the sword that swept through Egypt
   'Ere Israel's sons were free,
As the stream that breaks its channel
   And dashes to the sea,

That mighty roar burst on us,
  And the earth reeled to and fro
With the wild lament of thousands,
  With mourning and with woe.

Through all the coasts of England
  It was a fearful night—
A night of doubt and horror,
  Of trembling and affright.
The waters boiled with caverned wind,
  The blast was thick with foam,
The very elements themselves
  Were battling for a home;
And through the shadows of the night
  Uprose the crested waves,
Like headstones in a field that held
  A myriad years of graves.
No fitful gust, no stop, no stay,
  No whispers now were there,
No dubious note of mystic tone
  Those warring forces bare;
But winds and waves and crags gave forth
  One long continued roar.
There had not been so fierce a storm
  For forty years and more.

It came—a low, dull murmur
  Along the tempest came,
A long, low sound that followed hard
  On the phantom of a flame.

G

And there were men who heard it,
　And stood with straining eyes,
And hearts that flew towards the spot
　Whence the light seemed to rise.
Again upon the waiting eye
　That flashing message broke,
And to the listening ear again
　That pleading murmur spoke.
Away! away! each moment
　Is fraught with a human life.
Now, who are they will be men to-day,
　And venture for the strife?
Now, who will dare the tempest
　On such a night as this?
Who loveth man for the sake of man,
　And will danger a life for his?

'Tis answered. Calm and steady,
　With hearts prepared they come,
Cast but one glance upon the storm,
　And one long look on home.

There is no regal splendour,
　No banner streaming far,
No thrilling deeds of high-drawn birth,
　To cheer them to the war.
No lovely maiden lights them
　To battle with her smile;
No trumpet flourish breaks the air
　For many a leaguered mile;

No nation waits with triumph
　To bring them home again,
Or tasks herself to find rewards
　For the remnant from the slain :
But there, within yon hollow,
　That hardly you can see,
Are wives and mothers weeping,
　And infants round the knee.
And all before is darkness,
　And all behind is fear ;
And the rising sob, but half suppressed,
　Mingles with words of cheer.

Dressed in their fishers' garments,
　A gallant band and true,
There stood they, nothing daunted
　That raging flood to view.
They looked on the roaring mountains,
　All white with angry foam,
And the prayer went up and a blessing dwelt
　In one long look on home.

That look was past, and bringing
　The lifeboat to the shore,
Each man stept boldly to his place,
　And firmly grasped his oar ;
And with a will she darted
　Right on the thundering tide.
Now Heaven preserve that boat and crew,
　And make it safely ride !

The fierce tornado saw them,
  And called on the waves to rise :
" These be the sons of men who dare
  Our empire to despise."
And fiercer still, and fiercer
  The awful tumult grew,
And faster rolled the deepening swell,
And furious the tempest fell
  On the devoted crew.

And once and twice and thrice again
  It bore them sternly back ;
But the strong arms leant and the stout oars bent,
  They parted on the track.
As a lion 'midst the hunters
  Who compass him around,
Upstarting from his noonday lair,
Breaks headlong through the circling snare
  And frees him with a bound,
So gallantly the lifeboat
  Swept through the raging spray,
And, like a conquering spirit, passed
  Along the hostile way.

She lay upon the waters,
  A ship that none could save,
One broadside turned to heaven,
  And one towards the wave,

Circled with broken timbers
　That pinnacled the sea,
And spars and shrouds and shivered masts
　And cordage floating free,
And angry foam and drowning men—
　A piteous sight to see.

She lay upon the waters,
　And every wave that passed
Just raised her up to meet the next
　That hurried on the blast.
And groaning joints and creaking bends
　In mournful accents told
How sternly broke each following stroke
　Unceasingly that rolled.

"The lifeboat!" "Ay, the lifeboat!"
　And blessings rose on high,
And fluttering sobs and shouts of joy,
　And many a broken cry.
And hands told one another,
　In long and close impress,
The depth of misery that had filled
　The hours of distress;
And eyes that erst unwetted,
　Wept like a little child,
And, looking down on eyes that loved,
　Spake happiness and smiled,

She paused but for a moment,
  As onward still she passed
To save a beaten wretch who clung
  Unto a broken mast.
And then again, in answer
  To piteous cries for aid,
Another and another life
  A glory round her made.

Yet even while she rescued,
  Still while she strove to save,
The demons of the storm spurred hard
  On the remorseless wave ;
And full upon her counter
  The hostile torrent smote,
And dashing on in frantic pride
The water poured from every side
  Into the gallant boat.

She quivered for a moment
  Before the angry main :
The hand of God was on her,
  She righted well again.
She righted well, and dashing
  But faster for the check,
Still nearer drew where clung the few
  Still lingering on the wreck.

Hard task it was, and weary,
  To get them safely down
'Midst breaking seas and sudden plunge,
And dashing timbers' fearful lunge,
  And nature's blackest frown.
But one by one descended,
  Till she could hold no more ;
Then, with a promise to return
Soon as they reached the destined bourne,
  They parted for the shore.

And lids were wet at parting,
  Though eyes looked back to smile,
And welcomed hopes that, scarce believed,
  Still cheered them for a while.
But from the few survivors
  Who must perforce abide
Burst forth a cheer that shook the winds,
  And thundered o'er the tide.
They knew the weak and helpless
  In the hand of God were safe ;
What care they now though tempests blow,
  And angry waters chafe !

The strong arms leant and the stout oars bent,
  The waters felt their force,
As onward right to the guiding light
  They set the homeward course,

And dashing o'er the billows,
    Approached the whitened strand,
Swept through the surges of the coast,
    And felt the welcome land.
Then, by the past undaunted,
    Again they dared the war,
Until the last survivor stood
    In safety on the shore.

The waters roared and the tempest blew,
    But louder round the throne
The blessings pealed from those whom Death
    Had counted as his own.
And, writ in tears of praises,
    Stampt with the seal of light,
Shone bright in heaven each glorious name
Who boldly through the tempest came
    On that disastrous night.

THE PRISON OF THE DANE.

In the year A.D. 787 the first of the Danish ships appears to have visited the shores of England. Some years prior to this the Saxons had learned from tales of travellers of a people whose homes were found amongst the creeks and waterways on the shores to the east of the Northern Ocean, but they knew little of that race which was afterwards to play so important a part in the history of our country. In the year above named, the crew of one of their ships landed on the coast of Dorset. The reeve of the shire, not knowing who or what manner of men they were, caused them to be taken to Dorchester that they might there render an account of themselves, and this they appear to have done in an unexpected manner, for we read that "they slew men." Within a very few years after this, not only the Saxons on the seaboard, but those far in the interior of the country along the east coast, right up to Northumbria, learnt by bitter experience who and what the Danes were. Callous plunderers, they had no pity for those whom they attacked. Men and women fell before them or were reserved for torture ; children were tossed from pike to pike, and girls were carried away into slavery. Harrying far and wide, they robbed monasteries and treasures, slew the priests at the altar, and carried fire and sword into the heart of the country. At first their attacks were made with the sole object of shedding blood and obtaining booty ; but afterwards "they were ready to ransack a province, and to return with their ships filled with goods from the homesteads of the

land kings, and they were equally prepared, if the chance came
in their way, to hold the land for themselves and send for their
families to join them in the new home across the sea."

At first, and probably at times afterwards, a few ships only
would dart down on the coast, and retreat with their plunder as
rapidly as they came ; but as years went on larger expeditions
were fitted out, and the mere foray of sea-robbers met by the
sheriff and those whom he could hastily gather together, was
changed into the invasion of an army to be opposed only by a
royal force.

Whether in small or large numbers, the Danes swept over the
sea in their long black ships, swan-necked, dragon-prowed,
driven along either by a bank of oars, or, when the wind was
favourable, by huge dark red sails. From the descriptions received, and from one or two examples lately unearthed, these
ships appear to have been half-decked, between sixty and seventy
feet in length, and from twelve to sixteen feet broad. They were
somewhat roughly made, the timbers in some instances only
lashed together or fastened with wooden pegs or forks. Drawing
only about three or four feet of water, they were capable of being
driven at considerable speed, and from their lightness could easily
be drawn up upon a beach or carried by the crew over shallows
when ascending inland waters. Round their ships, when they
disembarked and had drawn them out of the reach of the tide,
the pirates made a fortified camp, and chose out from among
themselves those to whom was allotted the duty of protecting
their means of return. To this camp, if they were opposed too
strongly, they could retreat, and from thence keep their enemies
at bay until they had pushed their vessels into the water and were
able to embark and sail away. Their manner was, after over-
coming any opposition offered, to seize such horses as they could
find, and then, after scouring the neighbouring country, killing,
burning, and robbing, they returned with their spoil to the ships.

Axes, clubs, brown shining swords, and long rough-handled
spears were their principal weapons ; while, in addition to such
other defensive arms as each one might carry, they in many

cases wore over or above the face the likeness of a boar's head painted in divers colours and hardened in the fire. Well skilled as they were in warfare, greedy for spoil, and ruthless in fight, it is not to be wondered at if the prayer went up from the whole of Britain, "Deliver us, O Lord, from the frenzy of the Northmen."

In those days the soldier was a robber, warfare was the noblest occupation of man, death in the field the only fitting end to life. But when their arms were thrown aside, the Danes seem to have been gentle and loving to their home ties, and filled with a weird poetry, partly the result of their natural disposition, and partly that of training and of surrounding circumstances. Winning their way through the gloom of tangled forests or on broken shores, they dreamt of elves and supernatural powers, and in the flash of the lightning and the roar of the thunder they recognized the majesty of Wodin, the ringing of the hammer of Thor. They knew, too, or felt that there had been a time when, in the first creation, all things had been bright and glorious, but that by the fatal power of the blind demon of war, Baldr, the sun-god, the spirit of joy and beauty, had been overthrown and laid in death in the lap of Hel. Whether it was part of an old legend, or whether it was the result of the mixture of the religion of "the White Christ" with that of the Norse gods, we do not know; but very beautiful is the description given by their writers of the fate which falls on the world in the twilight of the gods and the prophecy of brighter days. "The sword age, the wolf age is coming, when the love of money shall scatter murder and harlotry over the earth. The powers of evil will be unloosed; the gods themselves fall in the desperate death struggle; fire consume the tree of life, and the solid earth and the dimmed sun sink for ever in the ocean. But a greener earth will rise out of the sea, lighted up by a brighter heaven, and Baldr will ascend from Hel to reign over new gods and nobler men." [*]

---

[*] Prose "Edda," c. 49, 51. Pearson's "Early and Middle Ages," 156.

Of this higher part of the Danish nature the Saxons knew nothing. They only recognized their enemies as robbers and murderers; and it wants but little imagination to tell with what consternation " the track of the destroying bark " must have been marked by the inhahitants of the coast. From the watch-towers, standing on the heights, the fire-signal would ascend. All the goods that could be hastily collected would be sent along with the old, the women, and the children to the nearest place of defence, and the men would gather together in arms to defend their families and their lives from the blow of the enemy. Unity of action would be the only chance of safety, and the reeve or the headman of the district would give the necessary directions for the coming struggle. Such a place as an old British encamp-ment or mound thrown up for the purpose of protection, not only against the attacks of tribal foes, but also against those of the wolves in winter, would, if near enough, be utilized, and on the spot most likely to be chosen for the attack the Saxon Chief would post his little army.

The Danes did not always succeed; but we may be certain that in any case the fighting would be furious and their losses great. In such a case as that which I have endeavoured to describe, the successful Danes, too much weakened to venture inland, would retreat to their ships, with the intention of returning to their own country with such spoil as they had been able to secure.

Whether the effect of a roller wave, produced by sub-oceanic volcanic agency, even if aided by a simultaneous depression of the coast line, would be such as is stated in the concluding lines, I cannot tell. It may be that in the sudden inburst of water, followed by a certain amount of refluence, every tree and build-ing would be so completely destroyed or overthrown that no trace would be left of that which had been. But even if this be so, can we be surprised if the fishermen and coast-dwellers of old, having heard from their forefathers of an attack by the Danes on the old mound, desperately defended by the Saxon valesmen, and how the baffled pirates on their return murdered

the father and child in Hilda's Tower, connected these facts
with the submergence of the coast, and out of many scattered
details wove a legend which taught them and their children how
the murderers were cut off in the moment of their crime by the
sudden dispensation of Divine power?

I.

THERE is tumult in the valley, there is gathering on
    the height,
And hands and shaded eyes are strained toward the
    dawning light:
To the far away, where the coming day glides between
    main and sky,
And the sea-line catches the ray from beyond and
    flashes it on to the eye.
O'er sky and sea, o'er wood and lea, the glorious light
    is spread;
O'er the low lands that stretch to the south, and o'er
    the northern head.
There's not a breath upon the deep that lies so vast
    and still,
And scarcely speak the waves that break on the sand
    at the foot of the hill:
But not upon the hill-top are peace and silence found;
Through all the hamlets in the vale the warning calls
    resound.
And men, in sudden roused from sleep, rush up the
    mountain side
To where the Peel Tower rests in guard above the
    eastern tide;

And boys and wildered elders wait, or follow as they
    may;
And startled mothers snatch their babes and, weeping,
    kneel and pray.

IL

Around the watchers on the height the growing
    numbers stand :
Half clothed, half armed, with panting breasts, a wild
    and anxious band.
Quick question, quick reply,—the finger pointing o'er
    the sea,
And rugged locks tossed from the brow and backward
    floating free.
A long stern look; breath short and hard ; a silence in
    the crowd,
And a low murmuring sound that grows to words and
    cries aloud ;
As the true eye descries far off upon the distant
    main
The fearful messengers of death—the warships of the
    Dane.

III.

Still on the hill above the beach the ruined tower is
    seen ;
Still to the east the pathway winds through rocks and
    slopes of green ;

And still within the valley the earth upturned will
show
Relics and bones of warriors who died there long
ago.
But up the sloping strand, along the south side of the
height,
Have rushed the waves of ocean—the ocean in its
might;
And when the winds are silent, and the tide, all lulled
to sleep,
Clear and smooth, reveals to light the secrets of the
deep,
Still may you trace the outlined walls far down beneath
the wave—
The walls of Saxon homesteads wrapped in a crystal
grave.
And when the tide is running low, there, farthest from
the shore,
Are the lines of a broken circle, with green weed
covered o'er.
For many an age that circle unchangeable hath stood,
Save in the change of the tinted weed that grows
beneath the flood;
And still the toilers on the coast the ancient legend
know
Of the old tower that breaks the wave when the tide
is running low.

IV.

Up the vale on the rising ground
British hands had raised a mound
With triple banks embattled round,—
A tribal fort, strengthened anew
What time the Roman eagles flew;
  And then, as years rolled on,
Neglected now, and now repaired;
Cumbered with growth, then surface bared;
Reduced or lengthened in its range,
But losing still from every change,
  Till half its strength was gone.

V.

Short time for action.   To the Hold
In haste are sent the weak and old.
The elder halts on his oaken staff,
  With faint and bended head;
The mother bears her living babe,
  Or the treasures of the dead,
And, sobbing, calls her children round,
  And sends them on before,
Each burdened with a little load
  Clutched from the garnered store.
Cattle and carts with fruit and grain
Are driven over the threatened plain,
  'Midst mingled shout and cry.

'Midst barking of dogs, and clang of thong,
And tramp of feet from the hurrying throng ;
'Midst lowing of herds and bleating of sheep,
Onward they press toward the keep,
    The tumult rises high.
Onward they press ; and in the rear,
From every hamlet circled near,
Gathers in arms with sword and spear,
With daggers wrought from pointed bone,
With axe of steel and hatchet of stone,
    The little Saxon host.
Onward they press, and the goal is won
Ere yet beneath the noontide sun
    The Dane has trod the coast.

VI.

On the shore where the wrack is strown
Stands a tower of rough-hewn stone.
Half a thousand years of storm
Have dashed upon its massive form.
The broken waves their foam have sent
High o'er its topmost battlement.
Wave and wind and snow and rain
Beat on its bulk, but beat in vain.
All unfingered by decay,
Winter and summer, night and day,
    Found it and left it bare.

H

Time seemed to it a thing of nought,
And petty years around it wrought
   To leave it in despair.
And there, in strong but narrowed room,
Anlaf, the Saxon, made his home,
Warrior and chief. The valesmen heard,
And owned the guidance of his word.
Brave and wise and mighty of hand,
He led the council in the land.
Kindly and true, he freely gave,
Nor turned him from the meanest slave ;
And loved by freeman and by thrall,
Meted his equal laws to all.
Wealthy, as riches then were given,
His garners owned the gifts of Heaven ;
But richer in the child that grew,
With golden hair and eyes of blue,
   Beneath his tending love—
A gentle maiden, sweet and good,
Just dawning into womanhood,
Who knelt before her father's chair,
And blessed his toil and soothed his care,
Or sat and prattled at his side,
And sung to him at eventide,
   Like an angel from above.

VII.

When through the vale the warning rolled,
Hilda was sent to the British Hold ;

And Anlaf, seizing axe and shield,
Headed his warriors in the field;
And silence reigned upon the strand,
Save for the wavelets that lapped on the sand.

VIII.

Onwards still across the waters, sweeping with resist-
less sway,
Come the war-ships—comes the raven, ever croaking
for the prey;
Come the hearts that know no pity, come the swords
that never spare,
Come the feet beneath whose iron all is blackened,
burned, and bare.
Men and maidens fall before them, till the reeking
stream of gore
Fills for them the cup that mantles in the paradise of
Thor.
And the grating of the vessel-keels upon the flinching
strand
Like the poison of an adder runs through all the
sickening land;
From the oars in serried motion gleams the radiance
of the sun,
Gleams in fiercer glow from weapons that a hundred
fights have won,
Falls on clubs and dinted targets reddened with a
darker stain,
On the flashing helm of Guthrac, mightiest leader of
the Dane.

IX.

The ships were beached; the pirate host
    Arrayed in order due;
High o'er the midst in fatal boast
    The bannered raven flew.
The sun shone on the bird of death,
    And on its ground of gold,
Outborne upon the ocean's breath
    The flashing hues were rolled.
It flew, but not, as oft of yore,
    With beak and wings outspread,
As glorying in the battle's roar,
    And hungering for the dead;
But the wings seemed weak and listless,
    And weary the head and low,
And there was a sound as of mourning
    As the flag waved to and fro,
And he seemed as one who listens
    To the voice of the fatal call,
And sees from afar the portals
    That lead to Odin's hall.
Yet still he strained in earnest flight
    Towards the battle-field,
As a chief who would spend his failing might,
    And die beneath his shield.

X.

On that omen, dark and drear,
Gazed the host with looks of fear;
Men of war, they knew full well
The face of death when warriors fell.
Little they recked when the strife was high
Who should live or who should die—
All too strong their souls and brave
To heed the terrors of the grave;
But none so bold but his heart sank low
As on that augury of woe
    His upward glance was thrown,
And his eye turned to his neighbour's face,
And sought, nor sought in vain, to trace
    The doubts that marked his own.
But Guthrac spake: " The conqueror's soul
    Is wasted by delay,
The power of the raven's wing
    Faints for the lack of prey."

XI.

Then swords and axes flashed on high,
And loudly rang the battle-cry.
It seemed as though the mystic bird
That gallant shout of war had heard,
    And roused his strength again:
No longer drooping at his side,
His glossy pinions opened wide;

His head was raised, his straining beak
In wonted accents seemed to speak,
    And clamour for the slain.

XII.

" Forwards ! "   Again the shout upsprings,
The march is set, the armour rings,
The pillaged tower is left behind,
Across the broken shore they wind
With heedful tread, as men who know
To meet and foil an ambushed foe,
    If ambushed foe there be.
A needless care.   Nor human sound,
Nor low of kine, nor bay of hound
Is heard, nor seen a hostile band ;
And silence lies upon the land
    As moonlight on the sea.

XIII.

The nearest homesteads yield a prize
Of little worth to eager eyes ;
A few small loads of meal and grain
And rustic tools are all they gain,
As through deserted barn and hall
Their rushing footsteps echoing fall.
Then disappointment to the hand,
In anger brings the kindled brand,

And the strong fire roars its tale
Of spiteful fury up the vale.

XIV.

When first the Saxons saw their foes,
Nor word nor cry nor shout arose,—
    Such was the chief's command ;
But when in quick succession fell
Before the desecrating spell
The simple beauties love had wrought,
The homes to which that love was brought,
The porches twined with clustering flowers,
The labours of their peaceful hours,
Reddened in flame or lost in smoke,
A wild fierce yell of vengeance broke
    From all the patriot band.
And as the blackened volumes rolled
Up the long glen and past the Hold,
    O'er plain and wood and down
Rang man's deep curse and woman's cry,
While frightened children veiled the eye
    Behind their mother's gown.

XV.

That shout, that cry rang far and wide.
In accents hoarse the Danes replied,
And at their leader's signal drew
Round where the bannered raven flew,

And man by man and shield by shield
In order moved along the field,
And placed their flag and ranged the host
A bowshot from the Saxon post.

XVI.

The beams of the failing sun are shed
On the clouds that roll o'er the mountain head,
O'er the mountain rolling slow,
Rimmed with silver and with snow;
And the rise of the wind, with moan and wail,
Sweeps in gusts along the vale,
And still and again is heard the roar
Of the waves as they beat upon the shore.

XVII.

Then, as wolves upon the quarry,
  Pealing loud their battle-song,
Rushed the foremost of the Danesmen,
  Rushed the strongest of the strong,
Lightly bounded through the heather,
  Lightly bounded o'er the rill,
Crossed the banks, and stemmed the boulders,
  At the rising of the hill.
There was seen the sword of Eric,
  Oswald's ponderous axe was there;
There the iron mace of Baldur,
  Mighty nurseling of the bear.

On they come, the chief and warriors,
   Where their ward the Saxons keep ;
Darts are flying, men are dying,
   As they labour up the steep.
On they press, while still above them
   Rings the shouting of the foe ;
On they press, while still around them
   Gallant heads are sinking low.

Blood and groans and death behind them,
   Round them hurl of dart and stone,
Up they press, the living heroes,
   Heroes that the gods may own,—

XVIII.

Up, and in the shock of battle,
   In the war steel's blinding flash,
All unseen the distant lightning,
   All unheard the thunder crash.
On and back the battle surges,
   Till, with numbers overpressed,
Cloven is the shield of Eric,
   Fallen Oswald's dragon crest.
Backward driven, faint and bleeding,
   Baldur stumbles o'er the slain.
Hark ! the shouting—comes the rescue,
   Guthrac comes, nor comes in vain ;
Fresh upon the mingled tumult,
   Comes the fury of the Dane.

XIX.

Louder then the shouts of battle,
　Blow for blow and thrust for thrust,
Dane and Saxon sink together
　In the violated dust.
Backward borne, yet still defying,
　Broken in the desperate strife,
Not one Saxon foot is flying,
　Not one cry is raised for life.
Overborne, the bleeding warrior
　Flings his useless club away,
Binds his arms around his foemen,
　Drives his teeth into the prey,
Till the writhing coils are stiffened,
　Life out-trodden in the fray.
Still with dying men surrounded,
　Stained with blood from head to heel,
Still unwearied, still unwounded,
　Anlaf wields his fatal steel.
Hark! the Danes have won the fortress:
　Woman's scream and children's wail,
Shouts of victors, groans of victim,
　Bear afar the fearful tale.
God! is there no room for pity?
　Is the witness heard on high?
Demons hold the earth in terror,
　And the weak and helpless die.

XX.

Weary, wounded, armour broken,
   Blunted axe and failing hands,
All his kinsmen dead around him,
   Lone, undaunted, Anlaf stands.
Loud and louder roars the thunder,
   Tempest floods are falling fast,
When, amid the closing battle,
   Chief to chief they meet at last,
Axe to axe. The lightning's power
   Gleams on weapons poised to smite,
And the crashing blow re-echoes
   In the darkness of the night ;
Falls the blow as bolt of heaven,
   Guthrac's crest is rent in twain,
But the Saxon axe is shivered
   On the helmet of the Dane.
For a moment bent the warrior ;
   Then, with reeling limb and eye,
Rushed again upon the foeman,
   Raised once more his blade on high :
But ere yet that axe descended,
   Mustering all his failing breath,
With his clenched fist undefended
   Anlaf smote the blow of death,
And before that mighty war-stroke
   Mingled blood and bone and brain,
And the smiter and the smitten
   Fell together on the plain.

XXI.

Yet some escaped : the night and the storm
Have shielded many a shrinking form,
And the neighbouring thickets lend their aid
And the dark woods a darker shade.
The pillagers have ceased their quest,
And slowly turned them back to rest
To the trysting place beyond the rill,
Where the raven is floating still.
Few the numbers that are left ;
Of their mightiest chief bereft,
They must wait till the light shall tell
Who are they in strife that fell.
Sleep and death together reign
Over the living and the slain.

XXII.

'Midst the helpless band that prayed
Stood the chieftain's little maid,
Motionless, with straining eye,
Tearless in its misery :
Had it not been for her waving hair
She might have been a statue there.
Ever she gazed where Anlaf's crest
Towered high above the rest ;
She watched his blade as it rose and fell,
She heard his shout o'er the battle's swell ;

On him alone her looks were bent,
For him alone her prayers were sent,
As though he only bore the strife,
And in his fate was wrapped her life.
And when the Danesmen stormed the Hold,
And death and rapine round her rolled,
Still had she stood; but, borne along
In the fierce pressure of the throng,
And lost the hero of the fight
'Midst deepening gloom and driving flight,
Her spirit broken by the strain,
With one low fluttering sob of pain
Fainting she fell; and as she lay
The sounds of murder passed away.

XXIII.

The storm had ceased ere life anew
O'er the faint soul remembrance threw,
And bade the dreadful past arise
Once more before her swimming eyes.
And deeper still its record burned
Till, thought and consciousness returned,
Stamped the sad knowledge on her heart,
And bade her fill a daughter's part.

XXIV.

Where the shattered war is strown,
Where the dying writhe and groan ;

O'er the soil with blood embrued,
'Midst the corpses pierced and hewed
Hilda passed on ; nor sight nor sound,
Nor treacherous hold on the trampled ground,
Might check the instinct that possessed
And thrilled its power in her breast.
The pitying stars looked down to bless
The maiden in her loneliness.
Oft had she wandered, in days of old,
Up and down the ancient Hold,
Chasing her mates in girlish play,
Or culling the blooms of the summer day.
Well she knew the way to trace
Through all the mazes of the place,
And on in the strength of her will she sped
To where the bravest champions bled,
Where thick on the earth the harvest lay
As the wrack-strewed beach on a stormy day.
With throbbing heart and anxious hand
She searched among the silent band.
Some power Divine her footsteps brought
Where the latest strife was fought,
Her trembling fingers gently led,
And placed them on her father's head.

XXV.

" Not dead—not dead ! "   The broken cry,
Where hope itself is agony.

The hope that fills the soul with fears,
Dims the parched eye with rushing tears,
Till breaking on with sudden start
The life-blood strains the labouring heart,
And surges on through nerve and vein.
" Was dead, and is alive again."

XXVI.

The winds of night with cooling breath
Had stayed the coming foot of death.
Down by her father's side she knelt,
　O'erburdened by the weight of bliss,
And his returning spirit felt
　The loving touch, the tender kiss,
And faintly to that love replied,
　And spake in accents weak and low,
And blessed him that he had not died
　And left his darling to the foe.
Then, from her garments torn, she bound
And strove to close each open wound,
And filled a helm from a little tide
That welled unstained from the fortress' side,
And gave him drink, and sobbed and smiled,
As a mother o'er her child.

XXVII.

Then Anlaf spake. " We may not stay
Here on the Hold till break of day,

For the foemen that remain
Will count the dead and spoil the slain.
None will escape upon the field,
And scarce the wood can shelter yield.
Refuge know I only one
Where their vengeance we may shun.
In the deep cell of our sea-girt tower
We perchance can foil their power
Till the spoilers have left the shore,
And their voices are heard on the coast no more."

XXVIII.

Taught by his word, the maid with speed
Hath sought and found his tethered steed ;
And, aided by her loving strength,
Hath Anlaf raised his frame at length ;
But stern the strain on the faithless limb,
And the brain reeled round and the eye grew dim,
And hardly might he gain his feet,
And win with pain the waiting seat.
But the strain had loosed what the hand had bound,
And the bandage sank from the clotted wound,
And scarce can Hilda staunch again
The blood that dropped from the opened vein.
'Twere hard to tell how oft her care
The burden of his weakness bare,
As on, with heedful eye and tread,
Adown the glen the steed she led.

Far in the gloom the ships lay beached,
And the long strand before her reached.
Then, o'er the stony causeway passed,
She brought her father home at last,
Upheld the broken strength that freed
His burden from the patient steed ;
Then barred secure the oaken door,
And laid him fainting on the floor.

XXIX.

The dying star-song of the night sinks in the dawning
day,
And the dark-blue sheen is changed to green, and the
green fades into grey,
And the sleepers are roused from their slumbers, and
at last the Danesmen know
How few of all their numbers are left them by the
foe.
Few ; and their mightiest warriors lie cold in the
springing fern.
Short rede is in their council—no course but to return ;
But the spoils of war must be gathered, and the earth
piled over the slain ;
Never the kites of England shall batten on the Dane.
Still stands the heap in the valley—men call it
Guthrac's Mound—
Where the chieftain sleeps with his followers in silence
ranged around.

I

Then down the path with hearts of wrath they turn
    toward the shore,
Nor stop till where the causeway shows the deep red
    stains of gore,
And one by one those stains lead on till they come
    to the oaken door.
Then the murder fiend was wakened, and far across
    the strand
Echoed the thundering strokes that fell from axe and
    club and brand,
Till the strong gate was broken, and through the
    opening poured,
In the dread power of vengeance, the leaders of the
    horde.
No warrior stood to meet them.   A little girlish
    hand
Upraised unarmed a moment stayed the fury of the
    band.
" Oh, spare him, spare my father ! "   She clasps the
    leader's knee.
His hand is in her golden hair ; his blade is flashing
    free.
Stern fell the blow.   The tide of life poured from her
    smitten side,
And o'er her slaughtered sire she fell, and on his
    breast she died.

XXX.

And then,—there came no warning, no sign of the
coming woe;
The sun shone bright in the heavens, and the wind
was hushed and low,—
But the Spirit of God was moving, as of old, on the
face of the sea,
And nature waited in silence to know what the end
would be.
Then the great depths were troubled, and the waters
rose on an heap—
Rose at the Master's bidding as a giant aroused from
sleep;
And o'er the plain of the ocean, with white plumes on
its crest,
Awful in pitiless strength the giant wave rolled on to
the west,
And night closed on the tower as with a sullen roar
That mighty bank of water rolled up the fated
shore.
It rolled over sand and boulder, it rolled up the
sloping glen,
And its crest of white round the south of the height
hid the ruined homes of men;
And a feeble cry rose here and there from the surface
of the wave,
But that wave rolled on and the cry was gone, and
the living found a grave.

And never more on sea or shore the pirate host was
  seen,
And never more their ships shall ride upon the ocean's
  green ;
And wheresoever those waters went, o'er strand and
  shining plain,
The veil they cast as on they passed shall ne'er be
  drawn again.
But often o'er the silver sea at night will Hilda glide,
And sing again the blessèd songs she sang at the
  eventide.
Still in the tower are living souls, so the old legends
  say,
And captive there the murderers wait till the dread
  judgment day ;
And high above the wild winds' cry, when the storm
  is on the main,
Is heard the hopeless wail that rings from the Prison
  of the Dane.

THE OLD MAN'S TALE.

Ye know that I am old and weak, and that I soon
    must die,
For ye hear the halting footstep, and mark the wearied
    eye.
To you the day is warm and bright, the song-bird's
    voice is clear,
The world is beauty to the sight and music to the ear.
I cannot joy in the balm of spring that comes from
    o'er the lea ;
The very beating of my heart is burdensome to me.
I linger on the doorstep, yet scarcely feel the sun ;
I only know how long the course, the goal how nearly
    won.
I have beaten the world in the race of time, and,
    passing on before,
By God's own grace I'll find a place at His appointed
    door.

The day hath been to me, as now it is to all of you,
When a blessing came with the early rain, a blessing
    with the dew.

My heart was light, my eye was bright, my step was
    free and strong,
And my soul took in the broad fair world and turned
    it into song ;
The lark rose up before my feet; the cliffs, the sky,
    the sea
Had but one voice, the voice of joy, and ever sang
    to me.
Far-stretched and fair my lands were spread, and rich
    my yearly store,
And with a grateful hand I fed the hungry and the
    poor.
Within my home a holy ray in soft effulgence shone,
The gentlest heart beneath the day was wedded to
    my own ;
And years went on, and tiny feet around my hearth
    were heard,
And gentle prattlings soft and sweet as music of a
    bird ;
Between my knees, in infant grace, a little angel stood.
What wonder if my Maker's face to me was very
    good ?

'Twas first a scarcely noticed word, and then a doubtful
    tale,
A rumour told with bated breath, with trembling lips
    and pale ;
And then the talk of ancient men in converse deep
    and low,

And in the heart a heavy gloom, the harbinger of woe ;
And then a blight upon the land, like to that cloud
    of old,
That, spreading from a little hand, o'er all the heaven
    rolled ;
And then we knew that it must come. If it were
    given to man
The power to work on earth the wrath and fulness of
    his ban,
Oh, what a fearful doom had been on him whose
    serpent-sting
Struck down the life of peace between the people and
    the king !
We knew that it must come at last, so dark the times
    had grown,
So heavy on the nation's life the burden of the
    throne ;
So deep and rankling was the steel oppression's hand
    had driven,
So loud and sad the daily cry that rose from earth to
    heaven.
In vain we struggled with the Lord in vigil, fast, and
    prayer ;
The very sheath forsook the sword, and left it keen
    and bare.
We could not see them set at nought, and idly stand
    aside,—
The rights for which our fathers fought, for which our
    fathers died.

And with the charter sealed in blood, and by the
    champions' graves,
Could we deny our title good, and own our children
    slaves ?

So the dark night of civil war reigned o'er the
    trembling land ;
Her edicts were the cannon-bursts, her sceptre was
    the brand.
O God, it was a fearful price, ay, even to be free,
That fratricidal sacrifice, that weight of misery !
Beneath the royal standard fought the chiefs whom
    feudal pride
And long descent of lordly rule won to the tyrant's
    side ;
And single-hearted loyalty, that only asked to own
A thankless master, and to die unnoticed and unknown.
And wily priests their meshes spread, and gathered as
    their prey
Men who had learned to bow the head, to listen and
    obey.
A gallant host.   We fought and won.   'Twere need-
    less now to tell
The shouts and garments rolled in blood before the
    monarch fell.
Not unto us ; by Thee alone, O Lord, the right was
    weighed,
By Thee alone the conquest won : to Thee be glory
    paid.

As arrows hurtling from the bow, shot with a master's
skill,
Our lot it was to deal the blow, but it was Thine to will.

I look across the long-drawn space of parted years.
Once more
I see my father's ancient hall ; I see an open door.
The faces I have loved are there—the mother and the
child,—
With the sweet looks that warmed my heart as heaven
when they smiled.
The loving eyes are filled with tears. The parting
hour has come ;
I hear the sound of hoof and steel, the bugle and the
drum.
And as the tendrils to the staff round which their curls
are thrown,
I feel the little trembling hands that gather round my
own ;
I feel the little trembling hands that bind me as a chain,
And the soft touch that as a prayer entreats me to
remain.
The hour has come. Lip clings to lip. There is a
smothered sigh,
A broken chord within the heart, a last, a sad good-
bye.
The vision fades away, but thus in dreams I often see
Those faces full of tender love, that were so dear to
me.

The tale of love that could not die—that love is
　　living now ;
I feel their lips upon my cheek, their breath upon my
　　brow ;
The brightest angels in the sky to me in mercy
　　given,
That on my darlings' gentle wings I may be borne to
　　heaven.

I thought that I had found a friend, one whom my
　　soul could hold
Warm as a sunbeam in the heart, and pure as tested
　　gold.
How oft together have we held sweet converse by the
　　way ;
Together stemmed the tide of fight, together knelt to
　　pray.
He was the casket of my thoughts ; my hopes and
　　fears he knew ;
His life was prized above my own, for I believed him
　　true,
And stronger than a brother's claim the wondrous
　　links that bind
Two chosen hearts together in the brotherhood of
　　kind.
When sorely wounded he was laid I was his help and
　　shield,
What time fierce Rupert's charge was made on
　　Marston's bloody field.

The blows fell fast. I held my own till Cromwell
    turned the day,
And then we staunched his bleeding wounds and bore
    him from the fray.
We laid him on the heathery bed ; it seemed the bed
    of death,
So deep and sore his wounds had bled, so weary was
    the breath ;
And many a long and anxious watch my sleepless
    eyes have kept,
Until the fevered brow was cool, the burdened spirit
    slept.
For slowly came the wave of life back from that tide-
    less sea
Where sleep the woes of human strife in vast
    eternity.
He lived. The glow of wonted strength by daily steps
    returned,
And I—my heart received at length the guerdon it
    had earned.

'Twas night, and not a star was seen. So dense and
    broad the cloud,
Of some vast city of the dead it might have been the
    shroud.
The distant fires of the camp shone lurid through the
    haze,
And strangely marked the slumbering forms around
    the changing blaze.

I could not rest, I could not sleep, for thoughts and
  hopes and fears,
And readings from the roll of love that filled my
  bygone years,
So crowded through the fevered brain in wild and
  mystic race,
That sleep, though welcome, tried in vain to find a
  resting-place.
Scarce knowing where, with ample cloak across my
  shoulders cast,
O'er the soft turf of early spring all silently I
  passed.
There was no sound upon the plain, no sound upon
  the hill,
And, save the tumult in my brain, 'twas very dark and
  still.
My wandering footsteps paused at length beneath an
  ancient tree,
And there I struggled with my thoughts, and bade the
  soul be free.

There came two voices speaking low close to my
  resting-place,
Low, but so near that every sound my startled sense
  could trace.
Full well I knew the one. (It was so dark that none
  could see
The silent covered form that lay beneath the branching tree.)

Silent, I held my breath with pain, for every little
    word
That told the treason of a friend went through me
    like a sword.
Slowly they came ; they paused a while ; then slowly
    wended on,
Leaving the echo of their speech e'en when themselves
    were gone.
Such words !—and I had heard them all. Till then
    I ne'er had thought,
Foul as it was, how very foul the sin that Judas
    wrought.
It seemed as though the air was full of perjury and
    crime,
And Heaven was hidden from the world, and devils
    ruled the time.

I followed where the voices led as hunter stalks the
    deer,
The falling step no sound betrayed to wake the victim's
    ear.
With weapon bared I followed close.   At last so near
    I stood
I marvelled that they had not heard the pulses of my
    blood ;
Then, as they paused upon the heath, through all my
    heart there went
A feeling that to give it words the very sky had
    rent,

And on the tempter's head was hurled the fury of my
 sword,
And at my feet in blood he fell, and died before the
 Lord.

Round Thornton turned.   His sword was drawn ere
 yet a moment sped,
Ere yet my own, all dank with gore, had risen from
 its dead.
Perchance he might have struck me down, but ere his
 weapon fell
I spake and cursed him in that name that I had loved
 so well.
He stood as one that doubts his ear hath told its tale
 aright,
Then quickly turned without a word and vanished in
 the night.

The plot was spoilt, the victory won.   From east to
 western coast
Were heard the chants, were seen the arms and banners
 of the host—
The host before whose battle brow had horse and foot
 gone down,
And every power and link that bound the kingdom to
 the crown.

The fleetest steed is slow of foot, and hard the
 smoothest way
When love impatient aims the goal, still chafing at delay,

And thought speeds on its course before, and checked
    returns again
To urge the rowels' deeper goad, and shake the
    slackened rein.
The road was long. For many a mile each moment
    as it passed
Was numbered in a heart that wished that moment
    was the last,
That wished that moment was the last of all the
    tedious hours
That stood before the blessèd love within my homely
    towers.
At length, at length, another day, another setting
    sun,
My own would be my own again, and all my toil be
    done !

But then there came a nameless dread, an awful sense
    of fear,
Like his who in the visioned night felt God Himself
    was near.
There was no sound, there was no sight; and yet
    within my brain
I seemed to see a stream of blood, to hear a shriek of
    pain ;
And then, it was no mortal sleep that o'er my senses
    stole,
It was no mortal dream that stamped its impress on
    my soul,

But like the seer's inspired trance, that, passing time
and space,
Commands the days unborn to live, and meets them
face to face.

The long-drawn sweep, the terraced walk, the ivy-
painted hall,
The shadows and the lights that traced each casement,
door, and wall,
The kennel and the sleeping hound, the copse and
silent stream,
That in its flowing scarcely seemed to break the silver
beam ;
The grand old forest far away, the hill, the drooping vale,
All pictured in the light that shone so bright and yet
so pale ;
The broad white orb, the distant gems that glittered
in the sky,
The clear dark hue all infinite that mocked the search-
ing eye ;
The snowy flakes of peaceful cloud, pure as a soul
forgiven,
Like down that from an angel's wing still lingers in
the heaven ;—
I saw them all, as still as though a spirit had imprest
On all the everlasting seal of deep and holy rest.
There was a hand upon my heart ; I could not speak
or move,
But sat in silent prayer before the temple of my love.

My very charger felt the spell, and stayed his panting
  breath,
Like an image carved at midnight by the pulseless
  hand of death.

Then came a change. The moon was hid, the sky
  grew black with cloud,
And 'midst the bending of the trees the tempest
  screamed aloud ;
Then through the loopholes in the wall my eye caught
  here and there
A little light that rose and sank, and then a lurid
  glare.
It grew. By Heaven ! 'twas all aglow : a flame and
  bursts of smoke,
Like the dashing spray when a giant rock hath
  trembled at the stroke.
Tossed aloft and hurled abroad by the winds in their
  headlong might;
Gloom and blaze and blaze and gloom breaking the
  sceptre of night,
Spreading its poison o'er lintel and beam, bursting
  each window and door,
Gathering strength from destruction and death, and
  mocking the wind in its roar ;
And that fell hand was on my heart, and I sat as
  locked in steel,
As one that had not life to move, and yet had the life
  to feel.

There were voices that screamed, and struggling forms ;
and few, and but here and there,
Would strong men battle a path to life, blackened and
scorched, and bare,—
Few and faint, for e'en to the strong the fight was
hardly won.
Oh, woe for the old, and the weak, and the young, for
rescue there was none ;
And the flames still rose, and I strove in vain to turn
away my eye.
O God, or ease my maddened brain, or give me
strength to die !
Higher and stronger grew the flames, and I knew that
the doom was cast ;
No breath of life could hold its own within that fiery blast.
But even then—oh ! passing sweet—like a whisper
they seemed so near,
I heard the voices that I loved, soft and gentle and clear;
Yet I knew in the depth of my inmost heart that those
sweet accents came—
Near as they seemed—from the chamber of death,
from the midst of the belt of flame.
They uttered the words I had loved to hear on many
an earlier day,
When the mother trained the childish lips, and taught
them how to pray
Those blessèd words that angels bear rejoicing to the
throne,
The burden of the infant's prayer that Jesus makes
His own—

The words that I so oft had heard lisped at the
mother's knee ;
And now, as then, although in death, I heard them
pray for me.
And then the flames shot up to the clouds, and the
smoke rolled far and wide,
And as the roof fell crashing in I knew that they had died.

A grasp was laid upon my arm. 'Twas Thornton's
voice that spake
In low and hissing accents like a serpent in the brake :
" Fool to instruct the hand that time or chance may
make a foe,
How best to reach the life, and where to strike the
surest blow.
I wot the quittance of revenge is written fair and plain ;
Rase if thou canst the seal of blood." He spake, and
turned the rein,
And down the road and o'er the moor I heard his
courser's tread ;
Then a great void came upon my soul, as I were with
the dead.

I woke, and lo ! it was a dream, a vision of unrest,
The working of a wearied soul with hope and fear
opprest.
The blessèd sun was in the sky, the morn was bright
and fair,
And the sweet notes of the song-birds were ringing in
the air.

It was a dream.   The night was gone, yet like a veil
  unrolled
There stood between the day and me all that the night
  had told—
A leprous spot on memory's life no stream could wash
  away,
A record on the page of time plain as the light of day.

On, on! no mortal man could bear to rest with such
  a load
Of sinking hopes and rising fears.   We sped along
  the road.
On, on! no stop beside the stream, no loiter in the
  shade ;
My thoughts but led the path before, and well my
  steed obeyed.
Past moor and hamlet, town and dell, swift as the
  winter's wind,
The very echoes of our tread, we left them far
  behind,
Till sudden, on the latest steep, the foam-flecked rein
  I drew.
Below me was a blackened pile ; my dream was only
  true.

How time went on, and life came back, it lists not
  here to tell ;
Or how I gathered proofs of all I knew before so
  well—

Proofs, damning proofs, that bore the guilt red to the
    murderer's hand,
Or how I traced him to the port from whence he fled
    the land.
I followed as a sleuth-hound tracks his flying victim's
    tread;
No spot through which his feet had passed but there
    my vengeance sped.
O'er mighty seas and long-drawn wastes and woods
    I held the chase,
In many climes, through many tribes of stern and
    savage race.
Unchanged, 'midst changing times, my hate as when
    I first began;
The whole world was my hunting-field, my prey a
    fellow-man.

Ye know not, ye whose daily life is filled with daily
    cares,
Who in your labour entertain an angel unawares,
How foul a thing the soul will grow that through long
    years of time
Lives but to do one single act, and that one act a crime.
I thought not in my happier days thus to exist for hate
My life a gleam of distant blood, my labour but to wait.
Eye for an eye, revenge for wrong, was all my heart
    could know;
And God was nought unless He wrought damnation
    on my foe.

Say I was mad. 'Tis no less true. I lived as others
    live,
Who in the depths of sin have lost the power to forgive.

There's mercy for a living man, refuse it as he will;
The love that suffers him to live through life pursues
    him still;
E'en on the hardest heart there falls the dew of saving
    grace,
And falls and falls perchance at last to find a resting-
    place.
I know not how it came, but for a moment now and then
I felt as power were given to love and bless my fellow-
    men.
A moment, and it passed away, and deeper was the
    night,
The blackness of my erring soul, for that one ray of light.
It was but, at first, like a little gleam that shineth from
    afar,
As the fitful glow in the dead of night of a very distant
    star;
But it came, and again, as the tide from the ebb turns
    and returns to the shore;
I was a man, a broken man, but still a man once more.

The bow that hath too long been bent, unstrung its
    bend retains;
The ransomed captive long can show the fester of his
    chains.

I could not feel as others felt, nor join the mingling
  throng,
The busy world, the daily talk, the laughter and the
  song ;
Far, far away from man's abode, toward the trackless
  west,
I thought to learn the secret road that guides the soul
  to rest.

'Twas winter, and the world was bare, and thick and
  fast the snow,
And without the wind was howling as the trees went
  to and fro.
Within, the pine logs glowed ; my dog was sleeping at
  my side ;
The Book was open at the tale of how the Saviour
  died.
I read as one that readeth on, to whom the words are
  nought,
As one whose ears receive the sound, but cannot feel
  the thought ;
Yet there I sat still reading, and reading o'er
  again,
Striving as man to feel for God, but striving still in
  vain.
All cold and dead at heart, I closed the volume in
  despair,
Nor was there strength within the soul to seek relief
  in prayer.

The slumbering dog had heard a sound, and started
    from his rest,
With bending neck and eager eyes, white fangs, and
    angry crest.
So deep the growl 'twas scarcely heard above the
    tempest's roar,
As slowly from the hearth he strode up to the guarded
    door.
I seized a gun, and stood prepared. The voice of
    human kind,
So weak no wonder it was lost in the howling of the wind,
A pleading voice in English tongue. I cast the gun
    aside,
And strongly in a far recess the struggling mastiff tied.
The bolts were drawn, the door flung wide ; a traveller
    worn with cold,
A single, weary, ghost-like man, a grizzled man, and old,
With failing step ; he scarce had strength to answer to
    my call,
And raised a trembling hand to rest against the cottage
    wall.
He entered, and I closed the door, and led his faltering
    feet,
Half bearing him, he was so weak, and placed him on
    a seat,
Piled up fresh wood upon the hearth, and brought him
    drink and food,
And chafed his weary limbs, and strove to warm the
    frozen blood.

And then I gazed upon him, on his thin grey locks of
    hair ;
The poor, worn face, that told of years, of long, long
    years of care ;
His starting bones and sunken eyes. And like a dart
    of flame,
Flashed forth a well-remembered face, and lo ! it was
    the same.
The tempter to my very hearth had brought my long-
    sought foe,
Had given his life into my hand, and bid me deal the
    blow.

My blood was mad as the days rose up, those evil
    days of yore ;
A murderous hand was at his throat, and dashed him
    to the floor ;
Shrieking, I hurled him from his seat. He knew me
    as he fell ;
One little glance—a moment's glance—and nought
    remained to tell.
And a short low cry burst from him, a bitter, painful
    cry,
The cry as of a hunted beast that feels that it must
    die.
A pause. No human hand it was that stayed the lifted
    knife,
It was no voice of living flesh that pleaded for his
    life ;

But I heard the rush of angel wings swift darting
    through the air,
I heard again those voices that last were heard in prayer,
And a great light burst upon my soul as through an
    open door,
And I felt that heaven was nearer then than e'er it
    was before.
Slowly I spoke : "Thy crime was great, and I have
    waited long,
And every day hath deeper stamped the memory of
    wrong.
In all my ways, in all my thoughts, in visions of the
    night,
This hour reddened with thy blood hath been before
    my sight ;
These twenty years for this alone my soul hath cared
    to live,
And now that vengeance is my own, I feel I must
    forgive,
And for His love by whose sweet grace my soul from
    sin is shriven,
I say to thee ' Depart in peace, uninjured and for-
    given.' "
Forgiven ?   Ah ! how vain the thought; the word
    how strange and wild,
And he, the murderer of my wife, the murderer of my
    child !
I stood aside. He slowly rose, pale as the dead white
    snow ;

One choking sob he gave, and then, with faltering
    steps and slow,
Without a word, as one from whom all living hopes
    are driven,
Passed outward to that dreadful gloom that barred the
    face of heaven.

I closed the door.   His withered form was hidden
    from my gaze.
The fire within burned warm and bright.   I sat before
    the blaze,
And strove to think that I had done, obedient to the
    Word,
The whole commandment, and had won the blessing
    of the Lord.
Had I not spared my direst foe when he was in my
    hand?
Had I not checked the lifted blow and cast away the
    brand?
Had I not stilled the raging blood, wild as an angry
    sea?
Wherefore, my God, for all my good in love remember
    me.

The fire within was warm and clear.   I sat before the
    light.
Without were moanings wild and drear, the moanings
    of the night;

The snow was falling thick and fast.   No other refuge
    nigh,
The homeless in that fearful blast had but one home
    —to die.
And words seemed borne in every gust, in every fitful
    sound—
" What hast thou done ?   Thy brother's blood is
    calling from the ground."
Brother !   Could such a wretch as he for one brief
    moment claim
From man, and least of all from me, so near, so dear
    a name ?
But then a writing on the wall stood plain and dread
    to see :
" In that thou didst it not for him, thou didst it not
    for Me."

I could not rest.   But few short yards those faltering
    steps had sped ;
I found him all so cold and stiff it seemed as he were
    dead.
I bore him home, and many an hour with ever watch-
    ful care,
As mother tends her little one, I sat and nursed him
    there ;
And reason came again, and life, but all too weak to
    stay,
And from between these arms at last his spirit passed
    away.

He died, and blessed me as he died. Ay, there are
few who know
The mercy that is stored for him who can forgive
a foe ;
But few can tell how deep and pure the peace that
Heaven can send,
For who gives vengeance up to God makes God Him-
self a friend.

PHILIP LEE.

(Originally inserted in "Temple Bar Magazine," 1869.)

A BITTER and a stormy night ; the wind was keen and
    strong,
And the white foam flew as the wild gusts blew, and
    bore the waves along.
Athwart the sky, athwart the moon, the scud was flying
    free,
And the foam that dashed through the firmament was
    like the foam of the sea.
My heart was at one with the changing light and the
    shadows hurrying past,
With the sound of the waves as they rose and fell,
    with the wind in its lull and blast ;
For the blood of life was full and strong, and the
    world was all before,
And 'twas better to stand on the beaten strand than
    to sit within the door ;
And I cared not whither my steps were bent, so I was
    alone on the shore.

For the plunge of the tide, and the song of the gale,
    and the phantoms of the mind,
Little I recked as I moved along how the waves rolled
    up behind.
Foot by foot they followed me close, as a lion that
    stalks his prey ;
One by one the marks I had left in the sand were
    washed away ;
Until I found I was compassed round with the cliffs
    and the boiling tide,
The heights behind and the waves before, and death
    on every side.
Stern and grand, and on either hand rounding out to
    the sea,
The broad cliffs raised their heads so high they could
    not care for me.
With a spring and a roar the waves rushed in, as a
    tiger that stretches his chain,
And for every check came thundering on with a
    spring and a roar again.
No kindly ledge, no winding path, nought but the
    pale blank wall ;
No sound but the whirl of the mocking winds and the
    waves in their rise and fall—
The pitiless waves ; and there was none but God on
    whom to call.

To wait and watch the shadow of death as it cometh
    on and on,

With none to bless the parting breath or weep when
the spirit is gone ;
To die like a dog without a word save only the broken
prayer
That cometh not from the heart of faith, but the
gasping of despair ;
With the cold sea-spray, like a serpent's slime, wreath-
ing o'er body and limb,
Till the heart is faint and the brain swims round, and
the sight is bleared and dim ;
With never a hope that God will hear, or, hearing,
heed the cry ;
To be beaten down with the doom of hell even before
I die ;—
I had not thought so deep a curse had been beneath
the sky.

Weary, weary in heart and brain, drenched, and
stiffened, and numb,
On a broken rock beneath the cliff I waited till death
should come,
Closed in between the rock and the cliff, or I had
been swept to the sea ;
For the broad stone quivered at every stroke, and
the waves came over my knee.
Soft and low, dreamy and slow, as the toll of a distant
bell,
To and fro the pulses go like the sea in its summer
swell,—

So gentle and slow the ebb and flow I might have
    been counted as dead,
So weak and loose the chain of life, it seemed that the
    spirit had fled.

A shout and a cry from the cliffs on high, twice, and
    thrice, and again,—
A shout and a hail above the gale, above the roar of
    the main.
'Twas heard, but I answered not, nor moved from the
    spot whereon I lay,
For it seemed to me, in my lethargy, as if life had
    wearied away;
It seemed to me, in my lethargy, that I lay beneath the
    wave,
And 'twas only the cry of a dying wretch as he joined
    me in the grave ;
And it was but at first like a little spot of rain on
    a summer day,
Scarce noticed, or perchance forgot ere it hath passed
    away.
But breathed anew it gathered strength, and would
    not be denied,
And I heard again the whirl of the wind, and the roar
    and the dash of the tide.
It was a bitter agony to feel that I had not died.

A moment, and again the shout down from the hill-top
    came,

L

And I heard and knew my father's voice as he called
    me by my name ;
And straight above me, bending o'er the margin of the
    height,
Were faces of men, like stars of God, all in the clear
    moonlight :
And the love of life came over my heart as a spring in
    a thirsty land,
And I strove to answer them back again, and feebly
    raised my hand.
" He lives ! " And I heard the shout of joy ; but
    mingled with the rest
Was a cry like the sob of a weary child as it sinks on
    its mother's breast ;
A cry that burst from a heart o'erstrained with the
    burden of its care,
And hurried from the quivering lips in mingled praise
    and prayer.

" Mine is the task," said Philip Lee ; " for though your
    heart is bold,
The cliff is high, and the wind is strong, and you are
    weak and old ;
My eye is clear, my arms are young, my life is bound
    to none,
And for the holy love of God I go to help your
    son."
They brought the rope ; with careful heed he bound
    it round his breast ;

And with a blessing and a prayer they launched him
  o'er the crest.
It was fending of foot and arm and hand as he swung
  there to and fro
In the whirl of the wind, with the rocks and the sea
  a hundred feet below.
"Steadily! Steadily! Lower again!" And longer
  grew the line,
Till he stood beside me under the cliff, and placed
  a hand on mine.

Higher and higher, the run of the tide came almost
  over the stone,
As he loosed the rope from off his waist and passed it
  round my own,
And fixed a slender cord to guide. Then, as a mother
  bends
To raise and bless the helpless babe that lovingly she
  tends,
He stooped and raised me tenderly, and for a moment
  stood,
And in his strength he held me up above the dashing
  flood.
"Ready?"—above. "Ready!"—below. "The time
  is short," said he,
"But even as I have kept faith with thine will God
  keep faith with me."
Then I was raised in the midnight air, and he was left
  in the sea.

My weakened sense went round and round ; I felt
and knew no more,
But still I seemed as one that hath dreamed of death
on a beaten shore ;
Till on the height in the moonbeams bright I opened
my eyes at last,
And knew that life had come again, and the dream
was in the past.
And I heard afar the song of the sea—it seemed but
a song to me then,
For the strong earth bore me up, and around were the
kindly tones of men.

Strong in hand and strong in heart, still holding to the
guide,
Philip had stood at the foot of the cliff in the tangle
and coil of the tide.
He guided me safe, though headlong waves behind
and round him broke,
And 'twas grapple of hand and grip of foot at each
repeated stroke.
In the bursting swell it was hard to tell the sea from
the mist of spray,
And the hungry waves, like living things, fought with
a living prey.
Yet still he held his purpose sure till o'er the dizzy
height
Kind hands stretched forth to take me in, and bore
me from his sight.

" Unloose the cords." The time is short; the battle
    is for life,
And none may abide in the rage of the tide, nor weary
    of the strife.
The knots are loosed; the cord is swung, and caught
    as it descends.
One struggle more and the fight is o'er, the victor with
    his friends ;
One struggle more and the fight is o'er. The rope is
    firmly bound.
" Ready?" But from below there came no answer to
    the sound,
But they heard a roar and a sullen plunge, and the
    spray dashed wild and free,
And they saw the broad white sheet of foam that lay
    on the angry sea,
And the light on the stone as the wave rolled back ;
    but where was Philip Lee?

The wave rolled back, but the knots held true. With
    drooped and bleeding head,
With mangled limbs all crushed and torn, and helpless
    as the dead,
A form was rescued from the wave. The very wind
    was still
As they raised him out of the boiling surf up to the
    crest of the hill.

Time passed away, but evermore Lee was a crippled
    man,

Weary and weak, as one whose years are broken in
their span.

Loving and loved of all he lived, loving and loved he
died,

The noblest, bravest, gentlest heart in all the country
side.

Then ask not why, when I shall die, I'll rest by Philip
Lee,

For well I ween that he hath been a neighbour unto
me.

SHORT PIECES.

HOPE.

Joys of the future, we hail your advancing
    Sunbeams of bliss in the mine of despair ;
Lights of the earth in the firmament dancing,
    Pillows of rest for the sickness of care.

What though the blast of the present be o'er us,
    Dark though the surges through which we have past ;
To-morrow's a haven of beauty before us,
    Filled with the joys that shall bless us at last.

When man from the Garden of Eden was driven,
    And Memory embittered his way with her tears,
It was Hope that directed his footsteps to heaven,
    And lit the heart fire that melted his fears.

Dead is the past, and the present is dying,
    Hope stretches its sceptre of life to the soul,
And all the dark shadows that round us are flying
    Are lost in the light that encircles the goal.

MARCH, 1862.

CAME a little sunbeam
　Floating on the morn,
Pure as words of heaven
　By an angel borne.

And we blessed the Giver
　For the gift He sent,
For the blessèd gift that came
　From the firmament.

It was half in heaven,
　Only half on earth ;
And we knew it clinging
　To its place of birth.

Yet our spirits trusted
　That its loving ray
Still would smile upon us,
　Even through the day ;

Hoped that it would warm us
  Even in the grave ;
So we blessed the Giver
  For the gift IIe gave.

Came a cloud of sorrow
  Rolling up the sky,
Came a mighty shadow,
  Came a wailing cry ;

And with eyes of weeping,
  Hearts bowed down with pain,
Looked we for the sunbeam ;
  But we looked in vain.

Still the cloud is o'er us,
  Still the gale is there ;
But it speaks no longer
  Accents of despair.

For we know the sunbeam
  Still is in the sky,
Though with beauty hidden
  From the mortal eye ;

Still it beams in Heaven
  But with brighter wave ;
Still we bless the Giver
  For the gift He gave.

CANA OF GALILEE.

IT was but water from the well,
　　But they filled the pots to the brim.
The duty that the Master taught
They questioned not, but simply wrought,
　　Obedient unto Him.

Put thou no value on the gift,
　　Give freely that is thine;
Unto the Master leave the rest:
Thine is but water at the best—
　　God turns it into wine.

THE LAND OF GOD'S DELIGHT.

I HEAR the angels whisper in the silent midnight air—
They tell me of another land where all is bright and
    fair,
A land of rest from struggle, of triumph after fight,
A land of joy and rapture, the land of God's delight.

Oh, lovely is the springtime, when the corn is young
    and green,
And the holy sunshine clothes the earth in robes of
    glowing sheen;
And glorious is the mighty sea, when winds and
    tempest cease,
And her broad bosom seems to be the home of God's
    own peace.

But lovelier far than any scene upon this world of
    ours
Is the sea before the emerald throne and the sheen in
    the heavenly bowers,

And sweeter far than any note upraised by mortal
tongue
Is the glorious song of praises by ransomed voices
sung.

Eye hath not seen, ear hath not heard, nor human
lips can tell,
The blessings God hath treasured up for those who
love Him well;
The bliss of those whom Christ Himself hath clothed
in robes of white,
Whose rest is found for ever in the land of God's
delight.

THE ANSWER TO "THE LAND OF LITTLE PEOPLE," BY F. E. WEATHERLEY.

YES; the land of little people is a lovelier land than ours,

With its mines of new-found treasures, mossy glades, and fairy bowers;

Earth her robe of choicest beauty spreads to woo the tender feet,

And the angels whispering round them thrill the air with accents sweet.

Memory brings no pang of sorrow, troubles lightly pass away;

Hope's horizon is to-morrow, and the sun is bright to-day;

Every moment has its blessing, sweeter thoughts, and fairer flowers.

Yes; the land of little people is a lovelier land than ours.

But from o'er the silent river comes to us a purer
    glow—
Purer even than the sunbeams that the little people
    know;
And the love-song of the heavens steals upon the
    wearied ear,
Sweeter than the angels' whispers that the little people
    hear;
And the wanderer overstriven, humbled as a little
    child,
Knows the past is all forgiven, and his God is
    reconciled,
When around his faltering footsteps comes the blessing
    of the dove,
From the fairest world of any, from the home of
    peace and love.

Brighter are the rays of morning that the dread of
    night is lost,
Dearer far the sheltering haven that the barque was
    tempest tossed;
And the simple child can never learn the beauty of
    that shore
Where the gloom of sin hath rested, where it resteth
    nevermore.
Weary feet may rest unsummoned, hopes downstricken
    rise again,
And the rainbow's glories sparkle on the far-off clouds
    of pain;

There are beauties aye unfading, gifts that Time can
ne'er recall,
For the country of the blessèd is the loveliest land
of all.

THE END.

PRINTED BY WILLIAM CLOWES AND SONS, LIMITED,
LONDON AND BECCLES.

A LIST OF

KEGAN PAUL, TRENCH & CO.'S
PUBLICATIONS.

11,87.

1, *Paternoster Square,*
London.

A LIST OF

KEGAN PAUL, TRENCH & CO.'S

PUBLICATIONS.

CONTENTS.

GENERAL LITERATURE.

A. K. H. B. — From a Quiet Place. A Volume of Sermons. Crown 8vo, 5*s.*

ALEXANDER, William, D.D., Bishop of Derry.—The Great Question, and other Sermons. Crown 8vo, 6*s.*

ALLIES, T. W., M.A.—Per Crucem ad Lucem. The Result of a Life. 2 vols. Demy 8vo, 25*s.*

A Life's Decision. Crown 8vo, 7*s.* 6*d.*

AMHERST, Rev. W. J.—The History of Catholic Emancipation and the Progress of the Catholic Church in the British Isles (chiefly in England) from 1771–1820. 2 vols. Demy 8vo, 24*s.*

AMOS, Professor Sheldon.—The History and Principles of the Civil Law of Rome. An aid to the Study of Scientific and Comparative Jurisprudence. Demy 8vo, 16*s.*

Ancient and Modern Britons. A Retrospect. 2 vols. Demy 8vo, 24*s.*

ARISTOTLE.—The Nicomachean Ethics of Aristotle. Translated by F. H. Peters, M.A. Third Edition. Crown 8vo, 6*s.*

AUBERTIN, J. J.—A Flight to Mexico. With 7 full-page Illustrations and a Railway Map of Mexico. Crown 8vo, 7*s.* 6*d.*

AUBERTIN, J. J.—continued.

Six Months in Cape Colony and Natal. With Illustrations and Map. Crown 8vo, 6s.

Aucassin and Nicolette. Edited in Old 'French and rendered in Modern English by F. W. BOURDILLON. Fcap 8vo, 7s. 6d.

AUCHMUTY, A. C.—**Dives and Pauper, and other Sermons.** Crown 8vo, 3s. 6d.

AZARIUS, Brother.—**Aristotle and the Christian Church.** Small crown 8vo, 3s. 6d.

BADGER, George Percy, D.C.L.—**An English-Arabic Lexicon.** In which the equivalent for English Words and Idiomatic Sentences are rendered into literary and colloquial Arabic. Royal 4to, 80s.

BAGEHOT, Walter.—**The English Constitution.** Fourth Edition. Crown 8vo, 7s. 6d.

Lombard Street. A Description of the Money Market. Eighth' Edition. Crown 8vo, 7s. 6d.

Essays on Parliamentary Reform. Crown 8vo, 5s.

Some Articles on the Depreciation of Silver, and Topics connected with it. Demy 8vo, 5s.

BAGOT, Alan, C.E.—**Accidents in Mines:** their Causes and Prevention. Crown 8vo, 6s.

The Principles of Colliery Ventilation. Second Edition, greatly enlarged. Crown 8vo, 5s.

The Principles of Civil Engineering as applied to Agriculture and Estate Management. Crown 8vo, 7s. 6d.

BAIRD, Henry M.—**The Huguenots and Henry of Navarre.** 2 vols. With Maps. 8vo, 24s.

BALDWIN, Capt. J. H.—**The Large and Small Game of Bengal and the North-Western Provinces of India.** With 20 Illustrations. New and Cheaper Edition. Small 4to, 10s. 6d.

BALL, John, F.R.S.—**Notes of a Naturalist in South America.** With Map. Crown 8vo, 8s. 6d.

BALLIN, Ada S. and F. L.—**A Hebrew Grammar.** With Exercises selected from the Bible. Crown 8vo, 7s. 6d.

BARCLAY, Edgar.—**Mountain Life in Algeria.** With numerous Illustrations by Photogravure. Crown 4to, 16s.

BASU, K. P., M.A.—**Students' Mathematical Companion.** Containing problems in Arithmetic, Algebra, Geometry, and Mensuration, for Students of the Indian Universities. Crown 8vo, 6s.

BAUR, Ferdinand, Dr. Ph.—A Philological Introduction to Greek and Latin for Students. Translated and adapted from the German, by C. KEGAN PAUL, M.A., and E. D. STONE, M.A. Third Edition. Crown 8vo, 6s.

BAYLY, Capt. George.—Sea Life Sixty Years Ago. A Record of Adventures which led up to the Discovery of the Relics of the long-missing Expedition commanded by the Comte de la Perouse. Crown 8vo, 3s. 6d.

BENSON, A. C.—William Laud, sometime Archbishop of Canterbury. A Study. With Portrait. Crown 8vo, 6s.

BIRD, Charles, F.G.S.—Higher Education in Germany and England. Small crown 8vo, 2s. 6d.

Birth and Growth of Religion. A Book for Workers. Crown 8vo, cloth, 2s. ; paper covers, 1s.

BLACKBURN, Mrs. Hugh.—Bible Beasts and Birds. 22 Illustrations of Scripture photographed from the Original. 4to, 42s.

BLECKLY, Henry.—Socrates and the Athenians : An Apology. Crown 8vo, 2s. 6d.

BLOOMFIELD, The Lady.—Reminiscences of Court and Diplomatic Life. New and Cheaper Edition. With Frontispiece. Crown 8vo, 6s.

BLUNT, The Ven. Archdeacon.—The Divine Patriot, and other Sermons. Preached in Scarborough and in Cannes. New and Cheaper Edition. Crown 8vo, 4s. 6d.

BLUNT, Wilfrid S.—The Future of Islam. Crown 8vo, 6s.

Ideas about India. Crown 8vo. Cloth, 6s.

BODDY, Alexander A.—To Kairwân the Holy. Scenes in Muhammedan Africa. With Route Map, and Eight Illustrations by A. F. JACASSEY. Crown 8vo, 6s.

BOSANQUET, Bernard.—Knowledge and Reality. A Criticism of Mr. F. H. Bradley's " Principles of Logic." Crown 8vo, 9s.

BOUVERIE-PUSEY, S. E. B.—Permanence and Evolution. An Inquiry into the Supposed Mutability of Animal Types. Crown 8vo, 5s.

BOWEN, H. C., M.A.—Studies in English. For the use of Modern Schools. Ninth Thousand. Small crown 8vo, 1s. 6d.

English Grammar for Beginners. Fcap. 8vo, 1s.

Simple English Poems. English Literature for Junior Classes. In four parts. Parts I., II., and III., 6d. each. Part IV., 1s. Complete, 3s.

BRADLEY, F. H.—The Principles of Logic. Demy 8vo, 16s.

BRIDGETT, Rev. T. E.—History of the Holy Eucharist in Great Britain. 2 vols. Demy 8vo, 18s.

BROOKE, Rev. Stopford A.—**The Fight of Faith.** Sermons preached on various occasions. Fifth Edition. Crown 8vo, 7*s.* 6*d.*

The Spirit of the Christian Life. Third Edition. Crown 8vo, 5*s.*

Theology in the English Poets.—Cowper, Coleridge, Words-worth, and Burns. Sixth Edition. Post 8vo, 5*s.*

Christ in Modern Life. Sixteenth Edition. Crown 8vo, 5*s.*

Sermons. First Series. Thirteenth Edition. Crown 8vo, 5*s.*

Sermons. Second Series. Sixth Edition. Crown 8vo, 5*s.*

BROWN, Horatio F.—**Life on the Lagoons.** With 2 Illustrations and Map. Crown 8vo, 6*s.*

Venetian Studies. Crown 8vo, 7*s.* 6*d.*

BROWN, Rev. J. Baldwin.—**The Higher Life.** Its Reality, Ex-perience, and Destiny. Sixth Edition. Crown 8vo, 5*s.*

Doctrine of Annihilation in the Light of the Gospel of Love. Five Discourses. Fourth Edition. Crown 8vo, 2*s.* 6*d.*

The Christian Policy of Life. A Book for Young Men of Business. Third Edition. Crown 8vo, 3*s.* 6*d.*

BURDETT, Henry C.—**Help in Sickness—Where to Go and What to Do.** Crown 8vo, 1*s.* 6*d.*

Helps to Health. The Habitation—The Nursery—The School-room and—The Person. With a Chapter on Pleasure and Health Resorts. Crown 8vo, 1*s.* 6*d.*

BURKE, Oliver J.—**South Isles of Aran (County Galway).** Crown 8vo, 2*s.* 6*d.*

BURKE, The Late Very Rev. T. N.—**His Life.** By W. J. FITZ-PATRICK. 2 vols. With Portrait. Demy 8vo, 30*s.*

BURTON, Lady.—**The Inner Life of Syria, Palestine, and the Holy Land.** Post 8vo, 6*s.*

CANDLER, C.—**The Prevention of Consumption.** A Mode of Prevention founded on a New Theory of the Nature of the Tubercle-Bacillus. Demy 8vo, 10*s.* 6*d.*

CAPES, J. M.—**The Church of the Apostles:** an Historical Inquiry. Demy 8vo, 9*s.*

Carlyle and the Open Secret of His Life. By HENRY LARKIN. Demy 8vo, 14*s.*

CARPENTER, W. B., LL.D., M.D., F.R.S., etc.—**The Principles of Mental Physiology.** With their Applications to the Training and Discipline of the Mind, and the Study of its Morbid Conditions. Illustrated. Sixth Edition. 8vo, 12*s.*

Catholic Dictionary. Containing some Account of the Doctrine, Discipline, Rites, Ceremonies, Councils, and Religious Orders of the Catholic Church. By WILLIAM E. ADDIS and THOMAS ARNOLD, M.A. Third Edition. Demy 8vo, 21*s*.

Century Guild Hobby Horse. Vol. I. Half parchment, 12*s*. 6*d*.

CHARLES, Rev. R. H.—**Forgiveness,** and other Sermons. Crown 8vo, 4*s*. 6*d*.

CHEYNE, Canon.—**The Prophecies of Isaiah.** Translated with Critical Notes and Dissertations. 2 vols. Fourth Edition. Demy 8vo, 25*s*.

    Job and Solomon; or, the Wisdom of the Old Testament. Demy 8vo, 12*s*. 6*d*.

    The Psalter; or, The Book of the Praises of Israel. Translated with Commentary. Demy 8vo.

CLAIRAUT.—**Elements of Geometry.** Translated by Dr. KAINES. With 145 Figures. Crown 8vo, 4*s*. 6*d*.

CLAPPERTON, Jane Hume.—**Scientific Meliorism and the Evolution of Happiness.** Large crown 8vo, 8*s*. 6*d*.

CLARKE, Rev. Henry James, A.K.C.—**The Fundamental Science.** Demy 8vo, 10*s*. 6*d*.

CLODD, Edward, F.R.A.S.—**The Childhood of the World:** a Simple Account of Man in. Early Times. Eighth Edition. Crown 8vo, 3*s*.
    A Special Edition for Schools. 1*s*.

    The Childhood of Religions. Including a Simple Account of the Birth and Growth of Myths and Legends. Eighth Thousand. Crown 8vo, 5*s*.
    A Special Edition for Schools. 1*s*. 6*d*.

    Jesus of Nazareth. With a brief sketch of Jewish History to the Time of His Birth. Small crown 8vo, 6*s*.

COGHLAN, J. Cole, D.D.—**The Modern Pharisee and other Sermons.** Edited by the Very Rev. H. H. DICKINSON, D.D., Dean of Chapel Royal, Dublin. New and Cheaper Edition. Crown 8vo, 7*s*. 6*d*.

COLERIDGE, Sara.—**Memoir and Letters of Sara Coleridge.** Edited by her Daughter. With Index. Cheap Edition. With Portrait. 7*s*. 6*d*.

COLERIDGE, The Hon. Stephen.—**Demetrius.** Crown 8vo, 5*s*.

CONNELL, A. K.—**Discontent and Danger in India.** Small crown 8vo, 3*s*. 6*d*.

    The Economic Revolution of India. Crown 8vo, 4*s*. 6*d*.

COOK, Keningale, LL.D.—**The Fathers of Jesus.** A Study of the Lineage of the Christian Doctrine and Traditions. 2 vols. Demy 8vo, 28*s*.

CORR, the late Rev. T. J., M.A.—**Favilla**; Tales, Essays, and Poems. Crown 8vo, 5s.

CORY, William.—**A Guide to Modern English History.** Part I. —MDCCCXV.-MDCCCXXX. Demy 8vo, 9s. Part II. MDCCCXXX.-MDCCCXXXV., 15s.

COTTON, H. J. S.—**New India, or India in Transition.** Third Edition. Crown 8vo, 4s. 6d.; Cheap Edition, paper covers, 1s.

COUTTS, Francis Burdett Money.—**The Training of the Instinct of Love.** With a Preface by the Rev. EDWARD THRING, M.A. Small crown 8vo, 2s. 6d.

COX, Rev. Sir George W., M.A., Bart.—**The Mythology of the Aryan Nations.** New Edition. Demy 8vo, 16s.

Tales of Ancient Greece. New Edition. Small crown 8vo, 6s.

A Manual of Mythology in the form of Question and Answer. New Edition. Fcap. 8vo, 3s.

An Introduction to the Science of Comparative Mythology and Folk-Lore. Second Edition. Crown 8vo. 7s. 6d.

COX, Rev. Sir G. W., M.A., Bart., and JONES, Eustace Hinton.—**Popular Romances of the Middle Ages.** Third Edition, in 1 vol. Crown 8vo, 6s.

COX, Rev. Samuel, D.D.—**A Commentary on the Book of Job** With a Translation. Second Edition. Demy 8vo, 15s.

Salvator Mundi; or, 'Is Christ the Saviour of all Men? Tenth Edition. Crown 8vo, 5s.

The Larger Hope. A Sequel to "Salvator Mundi." Second Edition. 16mo, 1s.

The Genesis of Evil, and other Sermons, mainly expository. Third Edition. Crown 8vo, 6s.

Balaam. An Exposition and a Study. Crown 8vo, 5s.

Miracles. An Argument and a Challenge. Crown 8vo, 2s. 6d.

CRAVEN, Mrs.—**A Year's Meditations.** Crown 8vo, 6s.

CRAWFURD, Oswald.—**Portugal, Old and New.** With Illustrations and Maps. New and Cheaper Edition. Crown 8vo, 6s.

CRUISE, Francis Richard, M.D.—**Thomas à Kempis.** Notes of a Visit to the Scenes in which his Life was spent. With Portraits and Illustrations. Demy 8vo, 12s.

CUNNINGHAM, W., B.D—**Politics and Economics:** An Essay on the Nature of the Principles of Political Economy, together with a survey of Recent Legislation. Crown 8vo, 5s.

DANIELL, Clarmont.—**The Gold Treasure of India.** An Inquiry into its Amount, the Cause of its Accumulation, and the Proper Means of using it as Money. Crown 8vo, 5s.

DANIELL, Clarmont.—continued.

Discarded Silver: a Plan for its Use as Money. Small crown 8vo, 2s.

DANIEL, Gerard. Mary Stuart: a Sketch and a Defence. Crown 8vo, 5s.

DARMESTETER, Arsene.—The Life of Words as the Symbols of Ideas. Crown 8vo, 4s. 6d.

DAVIDSON, Rev. Samuel, D.D., LL.D.—Canon of the Bible: Its Formation, History, and Fluctuations. Third and Revised Edition. Small crown 8vo, 5s.

The Doctrine of Last Things contained in the New Testament compared with the Notions of the Jews and the Statements of Church Creeds. Small crown 8vo, 3s. 6d.

DAWSON, Geo., M.A. Prayers, with a Discourse on Prayer. Edited by his Wife. First Series. Ninth Edition. Crown 8vo, 3s. 6d.

Prayers, with a Discourse on Prayer. Edited by GEORGE ST. CLAIR. Second Series. Crown 8vo, 6s.

Sermons on Disputed Points and Special Occasions. Edited by his Wife. Fourth Edition. Crown 8vo, 6s.

Sermons on Daily Life and Duty. Edited by his Wife. Fourth Edition. Crown 8vo, 6s.

The Authentic Gospel, and other Sermons. Edited by GEORGE ST. CLAIR, F.G.S. Third Edition. Crown 8vo, 6s.

Biographical Lectures. Edited by GEORGE ST. CLAIR, F.G.S. Third Edition. Large crown 8vo, 7s. 6d.

Shakespeare, and other Lectures. Edited by GEORGE ST. CLAIR, F.G.S. Large crown 8vo, 7s. 6d.

DE JONCOURT, Madame Marie.—Wholesome Cookery. Fourth Edition. Crown 8vo, cloth, 1s. 6d; paper covers, 1s.

DENT, H. C.—A Year in Brazil. With Notes on Religion, Meteorology, Natural History, etc. Maps and Illustrations. Demy 8vo, 18s.

Doctor Faust. The Old German Puppet Play, turned into English, with Introduction, etc., by T. C. H. HEDDERWICK. Large post 8vo, 7s. 6d.

DOWDEN, Edward, LL.D.—Shakspere: a Critical Study of his Mind and Art. Eighth Edition. Post 8vo, 12s.

Studies in Literature, 1789–1877. Fourth Edition. Large post 8vo, 6s.

Transcripts and Studies. Large post 8vo.

Dulce Domum. Fcap. 8vo, 5s.

DU MONCEL, Count.—The Telephone, the Microphone, and the Phonograph. With 74 Illustrations. Third Edition. Small crown 8vo, 5*s.*'

DUNN, H. Percy.—Infant Health. The Physiology and Hygiene of Early Life. Crown 8vo.

DURUY, Victor.—History of Rome and the Roman People. Edited by Prof. MAHAFFY. With nearly 3000 Illustrations. 4to. 6 vols. in 12 parts, 30*s.* each vol.

Education Library. Edited by Sir PHILIP MAGNUS :—

An Introduction to the History of Educational Theories. By OSCAR BROWNING, M.A. Second Edition. 3*s.* 6*d.*

Old Greek Education. By the Rev. Prof. MAHAFFY, M.A. Second Edition. 3*s.* 6*d.*

School Management. Including a general view of the work of Education, Organization and Discipline. By JOSEPH LANDON. Sixth Edition. 6*s.*

EDWARDES, Major-General Sir Herbert B.—Memorials of his Life and Letters. By his Wife. With Portrait and Illustrations. 2 vols. Demy 8vo, 36*s.*

ELSDALE, Henry.—Studies in Tennyson's Idylls. Crown 8vo, 5*s.*

Emerson's (Ralph Waldo) Life. By OLIVER WENDELL HOLMES. English Copyright Edition. With Portrait. Crown 8vo, 6*s.*

"Fan Kwae" at Canton before Treaty Days 1825–1844. By an old Resident. With Frontispiece. Crown 8vo, 5*s.*

Five o'clock Tea. Containing Receipts for Cakes, Savoury Sandwiches, etc. Fcap. 8vo, cloth, 1*s.* 6*d.* ; paper covers, 1*s.*

FOTHERINGHAM, James.—Studies in the Poetry of Robert Browning. Crown 8vo. 6*s.*

GARDINER, Samuel R., and J. BASS MULLINGER, M.A.—Introduction to the Study of English History. Second Edition. Large crown 8vo, 9*s.*

Genesis in Advance of Present Science. A Critical Investigation of Chapters I.–IX. By a Septuagenarian Beneficed Presbyter. Demy 8vo, 10*s.* 6*d.*

GEORGE, Henry.—Progress and Poverty : An Inquiry into the Causes of Industrial Depressions, and of Increase of Want with Increase of Wealth. The Remedy. Fifth Library Edition. Post 8vo, 7*s.* 6*d.* Cabinet Edition. Crown 8vo, 2*s.* 6*d.* Also a Cheap Edition. Limp cloth, 1*s.* 6*d.* ; paper covers, 1*s.*

Protection, or Free Trade. An Examination of the Tariff Question, with especial regard to the Interests of Labour. Second Edition. Crown 8vo, 5*s.*

GEORGE, Henry.—continued.

Social Problems. Fourth Thousand. Crown 8vo, 5s. Cheap Edition, paper covers, 1s.

GILBERT, Mrs. — **Autobiography, and other Memorials.** Edited by JOSIAH GILBERT. Fifth Edition. Crown 8vo, 7s. 6d.

GLANVILL, Joseph.—**Scepsis Scientifica ;** or, Confest Ignorance, the Way to Science ; in an Essay of the Vanity of Dogmatizing and Confident Opinion. Edited, with Introductory Essay, by JOHN OWEN. Elzevir 8vo, printed on hand-made paper, 6s.

Glossary of Terms and Phrases. Edited by the Rev. H. PERCY SMITH and others. Second and Cheaper Edition. Medium 8vo, 7s. 6d.

GLOVER, F., M.A.—**Exempla Latina.** A First Construing Book, with Short Notes, Lexicon, and an Introduction to the Analysis of Sentences. Second Edition. Fcap. 8vo, 2s.

GOODENOUGH, Commodore J. G.—**Memoir of,** with Extracts from his Letters and Journals. Edited by his Widow. With Steel Engraved Portrait. Third Edition. Crown 8vo, 5s.

GORDON, Major-General C. G.—**His Journals at Kartoum.** Printed from the original MS. With Introduction and Notes by A. EGMONT HAKE. Portrait, 2 Maps, and 30 Illustrations. Two vols., demy 8vo, 21s. Also a Cheap Edition in 1 vol., 6s.

Gordon's (General) Last Journal. A Facsimile of the last Journal received in England from GENERAL GORDON. Reproduced by Photo-lithography. Imperial 4to, £3 3s.

Events in his Life. From the Day of his Birth to the Day of his Death. By Sir H. W. GORDON. With Maps and Illustrations. Second Edition. Demy 8vo, 7s. 6d.

GOSSE, Edmund. — **Seventeenth Century Studies.** A Contribution to the History of English Poetry. Demy 8vo, 10s. 6d.

GOULD, Rev. S. Baring, M.A.—**Germany, Present and Past.** New and Cheaper Edition. Large crown 8vo, 7s. 6d.

The Vicar of Morwenstow. A Life of Robert Stephen Hawker. Crown 8vo, 6s.

GOWAN, Major Walter E.—**A. Ivanoff's Russian Grammar.** (16th Edition.) Translated, enlarged, and arranged for use of Students of the Russian Language. Demy 8vo, 6s.

GOWER, Lord Ronald. **My Reminiscences.** MINIATURE EDITION, printed on hand-made paper, limp parchment antique, 10s. 6d.

Bric-à-Brac. Being some Photoprints taken at Gower Lodge, Windsor. Super royal 8vo.

Last Days of Mary Antoinette. An Historical Sketch. With Portrait and Facsimiles. Fcap. 4to, 10s. 6d.

GOWER, Lord Ronald.—continued.

Notes of a Tour from Brindisi to Yokohama, 1883-1884. Fcap. 8vo, 2*s.* 6*d.*

*GRAHAM, William, M.A.—*The Creed of Science, Religious, Moral, and Social. Second Edition, Revised. Crown 8vo, 6*s.*

The Social Problem, in its Economic, Moral, and Political Aspects. Demy 8vo, 14*s.*

*GREY, Rowland.—*In Sunny Switzerland. A Tale of Six Weeks. Second Edition. Small crown 8vo, 5*s.*

Lindenblumen and other Stories. Small crown 8vo, 5*s.*

*GRIMLEY, Rev. H. N., M.A.—*Tremadoc Sermons, chiefly on the Spiritual Body, the Unseen World, and the Divine Humanity. Fourth Edition. Crown 8vo, 6*s.*

The Temple of Humanity, and other Sermons. Crown 8vo, 6*s.*

*GURNEY, Edmund.—*Tertium Quid : chapters on Various Disputed Questions. 2 vols. Crown 8vo, 12*s.*

*HADDON, Caroline.—*The Larger Life, Studies in Hinton's Ethics. Crown 8vo, 5*s.*

*HAECKEL, Prof. Ernst.—*The History of Creation. Translation revised by Professor E. RAY LANKESTER, M.A., F.R.S. With Coloured Plates and Genealogical Trees of the various groups of both Plants and Animals. 2 vols. Third Edition. Post 8vo, 32*s.*

The History of the Evolution of Man. With numerous Illustrations. 2 vols. Post 8vo, 32*s.*

A Visit to Ceylon. Post 8vo, 7*s.* 6*d.*

Freedom in Science and Teaching. With a Prefatory Note by T. H. HUXLEY, F.R.S. Crown 8vo, 5*s.*

Hamilton, Memoirs of Arthur, B.A., of Trinity College, Cambridge. Crown 8vo, 6*s.*

Handbook of Home Rule, being Articles on the Irish Question by Various Writers. Edited by JAMES BRYCE, M.P. Second Edition. Crown 8vo, 1*s.* sewed, or 1*s.* 6*d.* cloth.

*HARRIS, William.—*The History of the Radical Party in Parliament. Demy 8vo, 15*s.*

*HAWEIS, Rev. H. R., M.A.—*Current Coin. Materialism—The Devil—Crime—Drunkenness—Pauperism—Emotion—Recreation —The Sabbath. Fifth Edition. Crown 8vo, 5*s.*

Arrows in the Air. Fifth Edition. Crown 8vo, 5*s.*

Speech in Season. Fifth Edition. Crown 8vo, 5*s.*

Thoughts for the Times. Fourteenth Edition. Crown 8vo, 5*s.*

HAWEIS, Rev. H. R., M.A.—continued.

Unsectarian Family Prayers. New Edition. Fcap. 8vo, 1s. 6d.

HAWTHORNE, Nathaniel.—**Works.** Complete in Twelve Volumes. Large post 8vo, 7s. 6d. each volume.

HEATH, Francis George.—**Autumnal Leaves.** Third and cheaper Edition. Large crown 8vo, 6s.

Sylvan Winter. With 70 Illustrations. Large crown 8vo, 14s.

Hegel's Philosophy of Fine Art. The Introduction, translated by BERNARD BOSANQUET. Crown 8vo, 5s.

HENNESSY, Sir John Pope.—**Ralegh in Ireland.** With his Letters on Irish Affairs and some Contemporary Documents. Large crown 8vo, printed on hand-made paper, parchment, 10s. 6d.

HENRY, Philip.—**Diaries and Letters of.** Edited by MATTHEW HENRY LEE, M.A. Large crown 8vo, 7s. 6d.

HINTON, J.—**Life and Letters.** With an Introduction by Sir W. W. GULL, Bart., and Portrait engraved on Steel by C. H. Jeens. Fifth Edition. Crown 8vo, 8s. 6d.

Philosophy and Religion. Selections from the Manuscripts of the late James Hinton. Edited by CAROLINE HADDON. Second Edition. Crown 8vo, 5s.

The Law Breaker, and The Coming of the Law. Edited by MARGARET HINTON. Crown 8vo, 6s.

The Mystery of Pain. New Edition. Fcap. 8vo, 1s.

Homer's Iliad. Greek text, with a Translation by J. G. CORDERY. 2 vols. Demy 8vo, 24s.

HOOPER, Mary.—**Little Dinners: How to Serve them with Elegance and Economy.** Twentieth Edition. Crown 8vo, 2s. 6d.

Cookery for Invalids, Persons of Delicate Digestion, and Children. Fifth Edition. Crown 8vo, 2s. 6d.

Every-Day Meals. Being Economical and Wholesome Recipes for Breakfast, Luncheon, and Supper. Seventh Edition. Crown 8vo, 2s. 6d.

HOPKINS, Ellice. — **Work amongst Working Men.** Sixth Edition. Crown 8vo, 3s. 6d.

HORNADAY, W. T.—**Two Years in a Jungle.** With Illustrations. Demy 8vo, 21s.

HOSPITALIER, E.—**The Modern Applications of Electricity.** Translated and Enlarged by JULIUS MAIER, Ph.D. 2 vols. Second Edition, Revised, with many additions and numerous Illustrations. Demy 8vo, 25s.

HOWARD, Robert, M.A.—The Church of England and other Religious Communions. A course of Lectures delivered in the Parish Church of Clapham. Crown 8vo, 7s. 6d.

How to Make a Saint; or, The Process of Canonization in the Church of England. By the PRIG. Fcap 8vo, 3s. 6d.

HUNTER, William C.—Bits of Old China. Small crown 8vo, 6s.

HYNDMAN, H. M.—The Historical Basis of Socialism in England. Large crown 8vo, 8s. 6d.

IDDESLEIGH, Earl of.—The Pleasures, Dangers, and Uses of Desultory Reading. Fcap. 8vo, in Whatman paper cover, 1s.

IM THURN, Everard F.—Among the Indians of Guiana. Being Sketches, chiefly anthropologic, from the Interior of British Guiana. With 53 Illustrations and a Map. Demy 8vo, 18s.

JACCOUD, Prof. S.—The Curability and Treatment of Pulmonary Phthisis. Translated and edited by MONTAGU LUBBOCK, M.D. Demy 8vo, 15s.

Jaunt in a Junk : A Ten Days' Cruise in Indian Seas. Large crown 8vo, 7s. 6d.

JENKINS, E., and RAYMOND, J.—The Architect's Legal Handbook. Third Edition, revised. Crown 8vo, 6s.

JENKINS, Rev. Canon R. C.—Heraldry : English and Foreign. With a Dictionary of Heraldic Terms and 156 Illustrations. Small crown 8vo, 3s. 6d.

The Story of the Caraffa : the Pontificate of Paul IV. Small crown 8vo, 3s. 6d.

JOEL, L.—A Consul's Manual and Shipowner's and Shipmaster's Practical Guide in their Transactions Abroad. With Definitions of Nautical, Mercantile, and Legal Terms; a Glossary of Mercantile Terms in English, French, German, Italian, and Spanish ; Tables of the Money, Weights, and Measures of the Principal Commercial Nations and their Equivalents in British Standards; and Forms of Consular and Notarial Acts. Demy 8vo, 12s.

JOHNSTON, H. H., F.Z.S.—The Kilima-njaro Expedition. A Record of Scientific Exploration in Eastern Equatorial Africa, and a General Description of the Natural History, Languages, and Commerce of the Kilima-njaro District. With 6 Maps, and over 80 Illustrations by the Author. Demy 8vo, 21s.

JORDAN, Furneaux, F.R.C.S.—Anatomy and Physiology in Character. Crown 8vo, 5s.

JOYCE, P. W., LL.D., etc.—Old Celtic Romances. Translated from the Gaelic. Crown 8vo, 7s. 6d.

KAUFMANN, Rev. M., B.A.—Socialism : its Nature, its Dangers, and its Remedies considered. Crown 8vo, 7*s.* 6*d.*

Utopias ; or, Schemes of Social Improvement, from Sir Thomas More to Karl Marx. Crown 8vo, 5*s.*

KAY, David, F.R.G.S.—Education and Educators. Crown 8vo. 7*s.* 6*d.*

KAY, Joseph.—Free Trade in Land. Edited by his Widow. With Preface by the Right Hon. JOHN BRIGHT, M.P. Seventh Edition. Crown 8vo, 5*s.*

₊ Also a cheaper edition, without the Appendix, but with a Review of Recent Changes in the Land Laws of England, by the RIGHT HON. G. OSBORNE MORGAN, Q.C., M.P. Cloth, 1*s.* 6*d.* ; paper covers, 1*s.*

KELKE, W. H. H.—An Epitome of English Grammar for the Use of Students. Adapted to the London Matriculation Course and Similar Examinations. Crown 8vo, 4*s.* 6*d.*

KEMPIS, Thomas à.—Of the Imitation of Christ. Parchment Library Edition.—Parchment or cloth, 6*s.* ; vellum, 7*s.* 6*d.* The Red Line Edition, fcap. 8vo, cloth extra, 2*s.* 6*d.* The Cabinet Edition, small 8vo, cloth limp, 1*s.* ; cloth boards, 1*s.* 6*d.* The Miniature Edition, cloth limp, 32mo, 1*s.*

₊ All the above Editions may be had in various extra bindings.

Notes of a Visit to the Scenes in which his Life was spent. With numerous Illustrations. By F. R. CRUISE, M.D. Demy 8vo, 12*s.*

KETTLEWELL, Rev. S.—Thomas à Kempis and the Brothers of Common Life. With Portrait. Second Edition. Crown 8vo, 7*s.* 6*d.*

KIDD, Joseph, M.D.—The Laws of Therapeutics ; or, the Science and Art of Medicine. Second Edition. Crown 8vo, 6*s.*

KINGSFORD, Anna, M.D.—The Perfect Way in Diet. A Treatise advocating a Return to the Natural and Ancient Food of our Race. Third Edition. Small crown 8vo, 2*s.*

KINGSLEY, Charles, M.A.—Letters and Memories of his Life. Edited by his Wife. With two Steel Engraved Portraits, and Vignettes on Wood. Sixteenth Cabinet Edition. 2 vols. Crown 8vo, 12*s.*

₊ Also a People's Edition, in one volume. With Portrait. Crown 8vo, 6*s.*

All Saints' Day, and other Sermons. Edited by the Rev. W. HARRISON. Third Edition. Crown 8vo, 7*s.* 6*d.*

True Words for Brave Men. A Book for Soldiers' and Sailors' Libraries. Sixteenth Thousand. Crown 8vo, 2*s.* 6*d.*

KNOX, Alexander A.—The New Playground ; or, Wanderings in Algeria. New and Cheaper Edition. Large crown 8vo, 6*s.*

Kosmos ; or, the Hope of the World. 3*s.* 6*d.*

Land Concentration and Irresponsibility of Political Power, as causing the Anomaly of a Widespread State of Want by the Side of the Vast Supplies of Nature. Crown 8vo, 5*s.*

LANDON, Joseph.—**School Management ;** Including a General View of the Work of Education, Organization, and Discipline. Sixth Edition. Crown 8vo, 6*s.*

LAURIE, S. S.—**The Rise and Early Constitution of Universities.** With a Survey of Mediæval Education. Crown 8vo, 6*s.*

LEE, Rev. F. G., D.C.L.—**The Other World ;** or, Glimpses of the Supernatural. 2 vols. A New Edition. Crown 8vo, 15*s.*

LEFEVRE, Right Hon. G. Shaw.—**Peel and O'Connell.** Demy 8vo, 10*s.* 6*d.*

Letters from an Unknown Friend. By the Author of " Charles Lowder." With a Preface by the Rev. W. H. CLEAVER. Fcap. 8vo, 1*s.*

Life of a Prig. By ONE. Third Edition. Fcap. 8vo, 3*s.* 6*d.*

LILLIE, Arthur, M.R.A.S.—**The Popular Life of Buddha.** Containing an Answer to the Hibbert Lectures of 1881. With Illustrations. Crown 8vo, 6*s.*

Buddhism in Christendom ; or, Jesus the Essene. With Illustrations. Demy 8vo, 15*s.*

LONGFELLOW, H. Wadsworth.—**Life.** By his Brother, SAMUEL LONGFELLOW. With Portraits and Illustrations. 3 vols. Demy 8vo, 42*s.*

LONSDALE, Margaret.—**Sister Dora :** a Biography. With Portrait. Twenty-ninth Edition. Small crown 8vo, 2*s.* 6*d.*

George Eliot: Thoughts upon her Life, her Books, and Herself. Second Edition. Small crown 8vo, 1*s.* 6*d.*

LOUNSBURY, Thomas R.—**James Fenimore Cooper.** With Portrait. Crown 8vo, 5*s.*

LOWDER, Charles.—**A Biography.** By the Author of " St. Teresa." Twelfth Edition. Crown 8vo. With Portrait. 3*s.* 6*d.*

LÜCKES, Eva C. E.—**Lectures on General Nursing,** delivered to the Probationers of the London Hospital Training School for Nurses. Second Edition. Crown 8vo, 2*s.* 6*d.*

LYALL, William Rowe, D.D.—**Propædeia Prophetica ;** or, The Use and Design of the Old Testament Examined. New Edition. With Notices by GEORGE C. PEARSON, M.A., Hon. Canon of Canterbury. Demy 8vo, 10*s.* 6*d.*

LYTTON, Edward Bulwer, Lord.—**Life, Letters and Literary Remains.** By his Son, the EARL OF LYTTON. With Portraits, Illustrations and Facsimiles. Demy 8vo. Vols. I. and II., 32*s.*

MACAULAY, G. C.—Francis Beaumont : A Critical Study. Crown 8vo, 5*s.*

MACHIAVELLI, Niccolò. — Life and Times. By Prof. VILLARI. Translated by LINDA VILLARI. 4 vols. Large post 8vo, 48*s.*

Discourses on the First Decade of Titus Livius. Translated from the Italian by NINIAN HILL THOMSON, M.A. Large crown 8vo, 12*s.*

The Prince. Translated from the Italian by N. H. T. Small crown 8vo, printed on hand-made paper, bevelled boards, 6*s.*

MACNEILL, J. G. Swift.—How the Union was carried. Crown 8vo, cloth, 1*s.* 6*d.* ; paper covers, 1*s.*

MAGNUS, Lady.—About the Jews since Bible Times. From the Babylonian Exile till the English Exodus. Small crown 8vo, 6*s.*

MAGUIRE, Thomas.—Lectures on Philosophy. Demy 8vo, 9*s.*

Many Voices. A volume of Extracts from the Religious Writers of Christendom from the First to the Sixteenth Century. With Biographical Sketches. Crown 8vo, cloth extra, red edges, 6*s.*

MARKHAM, Capt. Albert Hastings, R.N.—The Great Frozen Sea : A Personal Narrative of the Voyage of the *Alert* during the Arctic Expedition of 1875-6. With 6 full-page Illustrations, 2 Maps, and 27 Woodcuts. Sixth and Cheaper Edition. Crown 8vo, 6*s.*

MARTINEAU, Gertrude.—Outline Lessons on Morals. Small crown 8vo, 3*s.* 6*d.*

MASON, Charlotte M.—Home Education : a Course of Lectures to Ladies. Crown 8vo, 3*s.* 6*d.*

Matter and Energy : An Examination of the Fundamental Conceptions of Physical Force. By B. L. L. Small crown 8vo, 2*s.*

MAUDSLEY, H., M.D.—Body and Will. Being an Essay concerning Will, in its Metaphysical, Physiological, and Pathological Aspects. 8vo, 12*s.*

Natural Causes and Supernatural Seemings. Second Edition. Crown 8vo, 6*s.*

McGRATH, Terence.—Pictures from Ireland. New and Cheaper Edition. Crown 8vo, 2*s.*

MEREDITH, M.A.—Theotokos, the Example for Woman. Dedicated, by permission, to Lady Agnes Wood. Revised by the Venerable Archdeacon DENISON. 32mo, limp cloth, 1*s.* 6*d.*

MILLER, Edward.—The History and Doctrines of Irvingism ; or, The so-called Catholic and Apostolic Church. 2 vols. Large post 8vo, 15*s.*

The Church in Relation to the State. Large crown 8vo, 4*s.*

MILLS, Herbert.—Poverty and the State; or, Work for the Unemployed. An Inquiry into the Causes and Extent of Enforced Idleness, with a Statement of a Remedy. Crown 8vo, 6s.

MITCHELL, Lucy M.—A History of Ancient Sculpture. With numerous Illustrations, including 6 Plates in Phototype. Super-royal 8vo, 42s.

MOCKLER, E.—A Grammar of the Baloochee Language, as it is spoken in Makran (Ancient Gedrosia), in the Persia-Arabic and Roman characters. Fcap. 8vo, 5s.

MOHL, Julius and Mary.—Letters and Recollections of. By M. C. M. SIMPSON. With Portraits and Two Illustrations. Demy 8vo, 15s.

MOLESWORTH, Rev. W. Nassau, M.A.—History of the Church of England from 1660. Large crown 8vo, 7s. 6d.

MORELL, J. R.—Euclid Simplified in Method and Language. Being a Manual of Geometry. Compiled from the most important French Works, approved by the University of Paris and the Minister of Public Instruction. Fcap. 8vo, 2s. 6d.

MORGAN, C. Lloyd.—The Springs of Conduct. An Essay in Evolution. Large crown 8vo, cloth, 7s. 6d.

MORISON, J. Cotter.—The Service of Man : an Essay towards the Religion of the Future. Second Edition. Demy 8vo, 10s. 6d.

MORSE, E. S., Ph.D.—First Book of Zoology. With numerous Illustrations. New and Cheaper Edition. Crown 8vo, 2s. 6d.

My Lawyer : A Concise Abridgment of the Laws of England. By a Barrister-at-Law. Crown 8vo, 6s. 6d.

NELSON, J. H., M.A.—A Prospectus of the Scientific Study of the Hindû Law. Demy 8vo, 9s.

Indian Usage and Judge-made Law in Madras. Demy 8vo, 12s.

NEWMAN, Cardinal.—Characteristics from the Writings of. Being Selections from his various Works. Arranged with the Author's personal Approval. Seventh Edition. With Portrait. Crown 8vo, 6s.

*** A Portrait of Cardinal Newman, mounted for framing, can be had, 2s. 6d.

NEWMAN, Francis William.—Essays on Diet. Small crown 8vo, cloth limp, 2s.

New Social Teachings. By POLITICUS. Small crown 8vo, 5s.

NICOLS, Arthur, F.G.S., F.R.G.S.—Chapters from the Physical History of the Earth : an Introduction to Geology and Palæontology. With numerous Illustrations. Crown 8vo, 5s.

NIHILL, Rev. H. D.—The Sisters of St. Mary at the Cross : Sisters of the Poor and their Work. Crown 8vo, 2s. 6d.

C

NOEL, The Hon. Roden.—**Essays on Poetry and Poets.** Demy 8vo, 12*s.*

NOPS, Marianne.—**Class Lessons on Euclid.** Part I. containing the First Two Books of the Elements. Crown 8vo, 2*s.* 6*d.*

Nuces: EXERCISES ON THE SYNTAX OF THE PUBLIC SCHOOL LATIN PRIMER. New Edition in Three Parts. Crown 8vo, each 1*s.*
*** The Three Parts can also be had bound together, 3*s.*

OATES, Frank, F.R.G.S.—**Matabele Land and the Victoria Falls.** A Naturalist's Wanderings in the Interior of South Africa. Edited by C. G. OATES, B.A. With numerous Illustrations and 4 Maps. Demy 8vo, 21*s.*

O'BRIEN, R. Barry.—**Irish Wrongs and English Remedies,** with other Essays. Crown 8vo, 5*s.*

OGLE, Anna C.—**A Lost Love.** Small crown 8vo, 2*s.* 6*d.*

O'MEARA, Kathleen.—**Henri Perreyve and his Counsels to the Sick.** Small crown 8vo, 5*s.*

One and a Half in Norway. A Chronicle of Small Beer. By Either and Both. Small crown 8vo, 3*s.* 6*d.*

O'NEIL, the late Rev. Lord.—**Sermons.** With Memoir and Portrait. Crown 8vo, 6*s.*

Essays and Addresses. Crown 8vo, 5*s.*

OTTLEY, H. Bickersteth.—**The Great Dilemma.** Christ His Own Witness or His Own Accuser. Six Lectures. Second Edition. Crown 8vo, 3*s.* 6*d.*

Our Public Schools—Eton, Harrow, Winchester, Rugby, Westminster, Marlborough, The Charterhouse. Crown 8vo, 6*s.*

PADGHAM, Richard.—**In the Midst of Life we are in Death.** Crown 8vo, 5*s.*

PALMER, the late William.—**Notes of a Visit to Russia in 1840-1841.** Selected and arranged by JOHN H. CARDINAL NEWMAN, with Portrait. Crown 8vo, 8*s.* 6*d.*

Early Christian Symbolism. A Series of Compositions from Fresco Paintings, Glasses, and Sculptured Sarcophagi. Edited by the Rev. Provost NORTHCOTE, D.D., and the Rev. Canon BROWNLOW, M.A. With Coloured Plates, folio, 42*s.*, or with Plain Plates, folio, 25*s.*

Parchment Library. Choicely Printed on hand-made paper, limp parchment antique or cloth, 6*s.* ; vellum, 7*s.* 6*d.* each volume.

The Poetical Works of John Milton. 2 vols.

Chaucer's Canterbury Tales. Edited by A. W. POLLARD. 2 vols.

Parchment Library—*continued.*

Letters and Journals of Jonathan Swift. Selected and edited, with a Commentary and Notes, by STANLEY LANE POOLE.

De Quincey's Confessions of an English Opium Eater. Reprinted from the First Edition. Edited by RICHARD GARNETT.

The Gospel according to Matthew, Mark, and Luke.

Selections from the Prose Writings of Jonathan Swift. With a Preface and Notes by STANLEY LANE-POOLE and Portrait.

English Sacred Lyrics.

Sir Joshua Reynolds's Discourses. Edited by EDMUND GOSSE.

Selections from Milton's Prose Writings. Edited by ERNEST MYERS.

The Book of Psalms. Translated by the Rev. Canon T. K. CHEYNE, M.A., D.D.

The Vicar of Wakefield. With Preface and Notes by AUSTIN DOBSON.

English Comic Dramatists. Edited by OSWALD CRAWFURD.

English Lyrics.

The Sonnets of John Milton. Edited by MARK PATTISON. With Portrait after Vertue.

French Lyrics. Selected and Annotated by GEORGE SAINTS-BURY. With a Miniature Frontispiece designed and etched by H. G. Glindoni.

Fables by Mr. John Gay. With Memoir by AUSTIN DOBSON, and an Etched Portrait from an unfinished Oil Sketch by Sir Godfrey Kneller.

Select Letters of Percy Bysshe Shelley. Edited, with an Introduction, by RICHARD GARNETT.

The Christian Year. Thoughts in Verse for the Sundays and Holy Days throughout the Year. With Miniature Portrait of the Rev. J. Keble, after a Drawing by G. Richmond, R.A.

Shakspere's Works. Complete in Twelve Volumes.

Eighteenth Century Essays. Selected and Edited by AUSTIN DOBSON. With a Miniature Frontispiece by R. Caldecott.

Q. Horati Flacci Opera. Edited by F. A. CORNISH, Assistant Master at Eton. With a Frontispiece after a design by L. Alma Tadema, etched by Leopold Lowenstam.

Edgar Allan Poe's Poems. With an Essay on his Poetry by ANDREW LANG, and a Frontispiece by Linley Sambourne.

Parchment Library—*continued.*

Shakspere's Sonnets. Edited by EDWARD DOWDEN. With a Frontispiece etched by Leopold Lowenstam, after the Death Mask.

English Odes. Selected by EDMUND GOSSE. With Frontispiece on India paper by Hamo Thornycroft, A.R.A.

Of the Imitation of Christ. By THOMAS À KEMPIS. A revised Translation. With Frontispiece on India paper, from a Design by W. B. Richmond.

Poems: Selected from PERCY BYSSHE SHELLEY. Dedicated to Lady Shelley. With a Preface by RICHARD GARNETT and a Miniature Frontispiece.

PARSLOE, Joseph.—Our Railways. Sketches, Historical and Descriptive. With Practical Information as to Fares and Rates, etc., and a Chapter on Railway Reform. Crown 8vo, 6s.

PASCAL, Blaise.—The Thoughts of. Translated from the Text of Auguste Molinier, by C. KEGAN PAUL. Large crown 8vo, with Frontispiece, printed on hand-made paper, parchment antique, or cloth, 12s.; vellum, 15s.

PAUL, Alexander.—Short Parliaments. A History of the National Demand for frequent General Elections. Small crown 8vo, 3s. 6d.

PAUL, C. Kegan.—Biographical Sketches. Printed on hand-made paper, bound in buckram. Second Edition. Crown 8vo, 7s. 6d.

PEARSON, Rev. S.—Week-day Living. A Book for Young Men and Women. Second Edition. Crown 8vo, 5s.

PENRICE, Major J.—Arabic and English Dictionary of the Koran. 4to, 21s.

PESCHEL, Dr. Oscar.—The Races of Man and their Geographical Distribution. Second Edition. Large crown 8vo, 9s.

PIDGEON, D.—An Engineer's Holiday; or, Notes of a Round Trip from Long. o° to o°. New and Cheaper Edition. Large crown 8vo, 7s. 6d.

Old World Questions and New World Answers. Second Edition. Large crown 8vo, 7s. 6d.

Plain Thoughts for Men. Eight Lectures delivered at Forester's Hall, Clerkenwell, during the London Mission, 1884. Crown 8vo, cloth, 1s. 6d; paper covers, 1s.

PRICE, Prof. Bonamy. — Chapters on Practical Political Economy. Being the Substance of Lectures delivered before the University of Oxford. New and Cheaper Edition. Crown 8vo, 5s.

Prig's Bede: the Venerable Bede, Expurgated, Expounded, and Exposed. By The Prig. Second Edition. Fcap. 8vo, 3s. 6d.

Pulpit Commentary, The. (*Old Testament Series.*) Edited by the Rev. J. S. EXELL, M.A., and the Very Rev. Dean H. D. M. SPENCE, M.A., D.D.

Genesis. By the Rev. T. WHITELAW, D.D. With Homilies by the Very Rev. J. F. MONTGOMERY, D.D., Rev. Prof. R. A. REDFORD, M.A., LL.B., Rev. F. HASTINGS, Rev. W. ROBERTS, M.A. An Introduction to the Study of the Old Testament by the Venerable Archdeacon FARRAR, D.D., F.R.S.; and Introductions to the Pentateuch by the Right Rev. H. COT-TERILL, D.D., and Rev. T. WHITELAW, M.A. Eighth Edition. 1 vol., 15s.

Exodus. By the Rev. Canon RAWLINSON. With Homilies by Rev. J. ORR, Rev. D. YOUNG, B.A., Rev. C. A. GOODHART, Rev. J. URQUHART, and the Rev. H. T. ROBJOHNS. Fourth Edition. 2 vols., 18s.

Leviticus. By the Rev. Prebendary MEYRICK, M.A. With Introductions by the Rev. R. COLLINS, Rev. Professor A. CAVE, and Homilies by Rev. Prof. REDFORD, LL.B., Rev. J. A. MACDONALD, Rev. W. CLARKSON, B.A., Rev. S. R. ALDRIDGE, LL.B., and Rev. McCHEYNE EDGAR. Fourth Edition. 15s.

Numbers. By the Rev. R. WINTERBOTHAM, LL.B. With Homilies by the Rev. Professor W. BINNIE, D.D., Rev. E. S. PROUT, M.A., Rev. D. YOUNG, Rev. J. WAITE, and an Introduction by the Rev. THOMAS WHITELAW, M.A. Fifth Edition. 15s.

Deuteronomy. By the Rev. W. L. ALEXANDER, D.D. With Homilies by Rev. C. CLEMANCE, D.D., Rev. J. ORR, B.D., Rev. R. M. EDGAR, M.A., Rev. D. DAVIES, M.A. Fourth edition. 15s.

Joshua. By Rev. J. J. LIAS, M.A. With Homilies by Rev. S. R. ALDRIDGE, LL.B., Rev. R. GLOVER, REV. E. DE PRESSENSÉ, D.D., Rev. J. WAITE, B.A., Rev. W. F. ADENEY, M.A.; and an Introduction by the Rev. A. PLUMMER, M.A. Fifth Edition. 12s. 6d.

Judges and Ruth. By the Bishop of BATH and WELLS, and Rev. J. MORISON, D.D. With Homilies by Rev. A. F. MUIR, M.A., Rev. W. F. ADENEY, M.A., Rev. W. M. STATHAM, and Rev. Professor J. THOMSON, M.A. Fifth Edition. 10s. 6d.

1 Samuel. By the Very Rev. R. P. SMITH, D.D. With Homilies by Rev. DONALD FRASER, D.D., Rev. Prof. CHAPMAN, and Rev. B. DALE. Sixth Edition. 15s.

1 Kings. By the Rev. JOSEPH HAMMOND, LL.B. With Homilies by the Rev. E. DE PRESSENSÉ, D.D., Rev. J. WAITE, B.A., Rev. A. ROWLAND, LL.B., Rev. J. A. MACDONALD, and Rev. J. URQUHART. Fifth Edition. 15s.

Pulpit Commentary, The—*continued.*

1 Chronicles. By the Rev. Prof. P. C. BARKER, M.A., LL.B.
With Homilies by Rev. Prof. J. R. THOMSON, M.A., Rev. R.
TUCK, B.A., Rev. W. CLARKSON, B.A., Rev. F. WHITFIELD,
M.A., and Rev. RICHARD GLOVER. 15s.

Ezra, Nehemiah, and Esther. By Rev. Canon G. RAWLINSON,
M.A. With Homilies by Rev. Prof. J. R. THOMSON, M.A., Rev.
Prof. R. A. REDFORD, LL.B., M.A., Rev. W. S. LEWIS, M.A.,
Rev. J. A. MACDONALD, Rev. A. MACKENNAL, B.A., Rev. W.
CLARKSON, B.A., Rev. F. HASTINGS, Rev. W. DINWIDDIE,
LL.B., Rev. Prof. ROWLANDS, B.A., Rev. G. WOOD, B.A.,
Rev. Prof. P. C. BARKER, M.A., LL.B., and the Rev. J. S.
EXELL, M.A. Sixth Edition. 1 vol., 12s. 6d.

Isaiah. By the Rev. Canon G. RAWLINSON, M.A. With Homilies
by Rev. Prof. E. JOHNSON, M.A., Rev. W. CLARKSON, B.A.,
Rev. W. M. STATHAM, and Rev. R. TUCK, B.A. Second
Edition. 2 vols., 15s. each.

Jeremiah. (Vol. I.) By the Rev. Canon T. K. CHEYNE, M.A.,
D.D. With Homilies by the Rev. W. F. ADENEY, M.A., Rev.
A. F. MUIR, M.A., Rev. S. CONWAY, B.A., Rev. J. WAITE,
B.A., and Rev. D. YOUNG, B.A. Third Edition. 15s.

Jeremiah (Vol. II.) and Lamentations. By Rev. T. K.
CHEYNE, M.A. With Homilies by Rev. Prof. J. R. THOMSON,
M.A., Rev. W. F. ADENEY, M.A., Rev. A. F. MUIR, M.A.,
Rev. S. CONWAY, B.A., Rev. D. YOUNG, B.A. 15s.

Hosea and Joel. By the Rev. Prof. J. J. GIVEN, Ph.D., D.D.
With Homilies by the Rev. Prof. J. R. THOMSON, M.A., Rev.
A. ROWLAND, B.A., LL.B., Rev. C. JERDAN, M.A., LL.B.,
Rev. J. ORR, M.A., B.D., and Rev. D. THOMAS, D.D. 15s.

Pulpit Commentary, The. (*New Testament Series.*)

St. Mark. By Very Rev. E. BICKERSTETH, D.D., Dean of Lich-
field. With Homilies by Rev. Prof. THOMSON, M.A., Rev. Prof.
J. J. GIVEN, Ph.D., D.D., Rev. Prof. JOHNSON, M.A., Rev. A.
ROWLAND, B.A., LL.B., Rev. A. MUIR, and Rev. R. GREEN.
Fifth Edition. 2 vols., 21s.

The Acts of the Apostles. By the Bishop of BATH and WELLS.
With Homilies by Rev. Prof. P. C. BARKER, M.A., LL.B., Rev.
Prof. E. JOHNSON, M.A., Rev. Prof. R. A. REDFORD, LL.B.,
Rev. R. TUCK, B.A., Rev. W. CLARKSON, B.A. Third Edition.
2 vols., 21s.

1 Corinthians. By the Ven. Archdeacon FARRAR, D.D. With
Homilies by Rev. Ex-Chancellor LIPSCOMB, LL.D., Rev.
DAVID THOMAS, D.D., Rev. D. FRASER, D.D., Rev. Prof.
J. R. THOMSON, M.A., Rev. J. WAITE, B.A., Rev. R. TUCK,
B.A., Rev. E. HURNDALL, M.A., and Rev. H. BREMNER, B.D.
Third Edition. 15s.

Pulpit Commentary, The—*continued.*

2 Corinthians and Galatians. By the Ven. Archdeacon FARRAR, D.D., and Rev. Prebendary E. HUXTABLE. With Homilies by Rev. Ex-Chancellor LIPSCOMB, LL.D., Rev. DAVID THOMAS, D.D., Rev. DONALD FRASER, D.D., Rev. R. TUCK, B.A., Rev. E. HURNDALL, M.A., Rev. Prof. J. R. THOMSON, M.A., Rev. R. FINLAYSON, B.A., Rev. W. F. ADENEY, M.A., Rev. R. M. EDGAR, M.A., and Rev. T. CROSKERY, D.D. 21*s.*

Ephesians, Philippians, and Colossians. By the Rev. Prof. W. G. BLAIKIE, D.D., Rev. B. C. CAFFIN, M.A., and Rev. G. G. FINDLAY, B.A. With Homilies by Rev. D. THOMAS, D.D., Rev. R. M. EDGAR, M.A., Rev. R. FINLAYSON, B.A., Rev. W. F. ADENEY, M.A., Rev. Prof. T. CROSKERY, D.D., Rev. E. S. PROUT, M.A., Rev. Canon VERNON HUTTON, and Rev. U. R. THOMAS, D.D. Second Edition. 21*s.*

Thessalonians, Timothy, Titus, and Philemon. By the Bishop of Bath and Wells, Rev. Dr. GLOAG and Rev. Dr. EALES. With Homilies by the Rev. B. C. CAFFIN, M.A., Rev. R. FINLAYSON, B.A., Rev. Prof. T. CROSKERY, D.D., Rev. W. F. ADENEY, M.A., Rev. W. M. STATHAM, and Rev. D. THOMAS, D.D. 15*s.*

Hebrews and James. By the Rev. J. BARMBY, D.D., and Rev Prebendary E. C. S. GIBSON, M.A. With Homiletics by the Rev. C. JERDAN, M.A., LL.B., and Rev. Prebendary E. C. S. GIBSON. And Homilies by the Rev. W. JONES, Rev. C. NEW, Rev. D. YOUNG, B.A., Rev. J. S. BRIGHT, Rev. T. F. LOCKYER, B.A., and Rev. C. JERDAN, M.A., LL.B. Second Edition. 15*s.*

PUSEY, Dr.—**Sermons for the Church's Seasons from Advent to Trinity.** Selected from the Published Sermons of the late EDWARD BOUVERIE PUSEY, D.D. Crown 8vo, 5*s.*

RANKE, Leopold von.—**Universal History.** The oldest Historical Group of Nations and the Greeks. Edited by G. W. PROTHERO. Demy 8vo, 16*s.*

RENDELL, J. M.—**Concise Handbook of the Island of Madeira.** With Plan of Funchal and Map of the Island. Fcap. 8vo, 1*s.* 6*d.*

REVELL, W. F.—**Ethical Forecasts.** Crown 8vo.

REYNOLDS, Rev. J. W.—**The Supernatural in Nature.** A Verification by Free Use of Science. Third Edition, Revised and Enlarged. Demy 8vo, 14*s.*

The Mystery of Miracles. Third and Enlarged Edition. Crown 8vo, 6*s.*

The Mystery of the Universe our Common Faith. Demy 8vo, 14*s.*

The World to Come: Immortality a Physical Fact. Crown 8vo, 6*s.*

RIBOT, Prof. Th.—Heredity: A Psychological Study of its Phenomena, its Laws, its Causes, and its Consequences. Second Edition. Large crown 8vo, 9*s.*

ROBERTSON, The late Rev. F. W., M.A.—Life and Letters of. Edited by the Rev. STOPFORD BROOKE, M.A.
    I. Two vols., uniform with the Sermons. With Steel Portrait. Crown 8vo, 7*s.* 6*d.*
    II. Library Edition, in Demy 8vo, with Portrait. 12*s.*
    III. A Popular Edition, in 1 vol. Crown 8vo, 6*s.*

ROBERTSON, The late Rev. F. W., M.A.—continued.
Sermons. Four Series. Small crown 8vo, 3*s.* 6*d.* each.

The Human Race, and other Sermons. Preached at Cheltenham, Oxford, and Brighton. New and Cheaper Edition. Small crown 8vo, 3*s.* 6*d.*

Notes on Genesis. New and Cheaper Edition. Small crown 8vo, 3*s.* 6*d.*

Expository Lectures on St. Paul's Epistles to the Corinthians. A New Edition. Small crown 8vo, 5*s.*

Lectures and Addresses, with other Literary Remains. A New Edition. Small crown 8vo, 5*s.*

An Analysis of Tennyson's " In Memoriam." (Dedicated by Permission to the Poet-Laureate.) Fcap. 8vo, 2*s.*

The Education of the Human Race. Translated from the German of GOTTHOLD EPHRAIM LESSING. Fcap. 8vo, 2*s.* 6*d.*
The above Works can also be had, bound in half morocco.

*** A Portrait of the late Rev. F. W. Robertson, mounted for framing, can be had, 2*s.* 6*d.*

ROMANES, G. J. — Mental Evolution in Animals. With a Posthumous Essay on Instinct by CHARLES DARWIN, F.R.S. Demy 8vo, 12*s.*

ROOSEVELT, Theodore. Hunting Trips of a Ranchman. Sketches of Sport on the Northern Cattle Plains. With 26 Illustrations. Royal 8vo, 18*s.*

ROSMINI SERBATI, Antonio.—Life. By the REV. W. LOCKHART. Second Edition. 2 vols. With Portraits. Crown 8vo, 12*s.*

Rosmini's Origin of Ideas. Translated from the Fifth Italian Edition of the Nuovo Saggio *Sull' origine delle idee.* 3 vols. Demy 8vo, cloth, 10*s.* 6*d.* each.

Rosmini's Psychology. 3 vols. Demy 8vo [Vols. I. and II. now ready], 10*s.* 6*d.* each.

ROSS, Janet.—Italian Sketches. With 14 full-page Illustrations. Crown 8vo, 7*s.* 6*d.*

RULE, Martin, M.A. — The Life and Times of St. Anselm, Archbishop of Canterbury and Primate of the Britains. 2 vols. Demy 8vo, 32*s.*

SAMUELL, Richard.—Seven, the Sacred Number: Its use in Scripture and its Application to Biblical Criticism. Crown 8vo, 10s. 6d.

SAYCE, Rev. Archibald Henry.—Introduction to the Science of Language. 2 vols. Second Edition. Large post 8vo, 21s.

SCOONES, W. Baptiste.—Four Centuries of English Letters: A Selection of 350 Letters by 150 Writers, from the Period of the Paston Letters to the Present Time. Third Edition. Large crown 8vo, 6s.

SÉE, Prof. Germain.—Bacillary Phthisis of the Lungs. Translated and edited for English Practitioners by WILLIAM HENRY WEDDELL, M.R.C.S. Demy 8vo, 10s. 6d.

Shakspere's Works. The Avon Edition, 12 vols., fcap. 8vo, cloth, 18s.; in cloth box, 21s.; bound in 6 vols., cloth, 15s.

Shakspere's Works, an Index to. By EVANGELINE O'CONNOR. Crown 8vo, 5s.

SHELLEY, Percy Bysshe.—Life. By EDWARD DOWDEN, LL.D. 2 vols. With Portraits. Demy 8vo, 36s.

SHILLITO, Rev. Joseph.—Womanhood: its Duties, Temptations, and Privileges. A Book for Young Women. Third Edition. Crown 8vo, 3s. 6d.

Shooting, Practical Hints. Being a Treatise on the Shot Gun and its Management. By "20 Bore." With 55 Illustrations. Demy 8vo, 12s.

Sister Augustine, Superior of the Sisters of Charity at the St. Johannis Hospital at Bonn. Authorized Translation by HANS THARAU, from the German "Memorials of AMALIE VON LASAULX." Cheap Edition. Large crown 8vo, 4s. 6d.

SKINNER, James.—A Memoir. By the Author of "Charles Lowder." With a Preface by the Rev. Canon CARTER, and Portrait. Large crown, 7s. 6d.
*** Also a cheap Edition. With Portrait. Fourth Edition. Crown 8vo, 3s. 6d.

SMEATON, D. Mackenzie. — The Loyal Karens of Burma. Crown 8vo, 4s. 6d.

SMITH, Edward, M.D., LL.B., F.R.S.—Tubercular Consumption in its Early and Remediable Stages. Second Edition. Crown 8vo, 6s.

SMITH, Sir W. Cusack, Bart.—Our War Ships. A Naval Essay. Crown 8vo, 5s.

Spanish Mystics. By the Editor of "Many Voices." Crown 8vo, 5s.

Specimens of English Prose Style from Malory to Macaulay. Selected and Annotated, with an Introductory Essay, by GEORGE SAINTSBURY. Large crown 8vo, printed on hand-made paper, parchment antique or cloth, 12s.; vellum, 15s.

SPEDDING, James.—Reviews and Discussions, Literary, Political, and Historical not relating to Bacon. Demy 8vo, 12s. 6d.

　　Evenings with a Reviewer ; or, Macaulay and Bacon. With a Prefatory Notice by G. S. VENABLES, Q.C. 2 vols. Demy 8vo, 18s.

Stray Papers on Education, and Scenes from School Life. By B. H. Second Edition. Small crown 8vo, 3s. 6d.

STREATFEILD, Rev. G. S., M.A.—Lincolnshire and the Danes. Large crown 8vo, 7s. 6d.

STRECKER-WISLICENUS.—Organic Chemistry. Translated and Edited, with Extensive Additions, by W. R. HODGKINSON, Ph.D., and A. J. GREENAWAY, F.I.C. Second and cheaper Edition. Demy 8vo, 12s. 6d.

Suakin, 1885 ; being a Sketch of the Campaign of this year. By an Officer who was there. Second Edition. Crown 8vo, 2s. 6d.

SULLY, James, M.A.—Pessimism : a History and a Criticism. Second Edition. Demy 8vo, 14s.

Sunshine and Sea. A Yachting Visit to the Channel Islands and Coast of Brittany. With Frontispiece from a Photograph and 24 Illustrations. Crown 8vo, 6s.

SWEDENBORG, Eman.—De Cultu et Amore Dei ubi Agitur de Telluris ortu, Paradiso et Vivario, tum de Primogeniti Seu Adami Nativitate Infantia, et Amore. Crown 8vo, 6s.

　　On the Worship and Love of God. Treating of the Birth of the Earth, Paradise, and the Abode of Living Creatures. Translated from the original Latin. Crown 8vo, 7s. 6d.

　　Prodromus Philosophiæ Ratiocinantis de Infinito, et Causa Finali Creationis : deque Mechanismo Operationis Animæ et Corporis. Edidit THOMAS MURRAY GORMAN, M.A. Crown 8vo, 7s. 6d.

TACITUS.—The Agricola. A Translation. Small crown 8vo, 2s. 6d.

TARRING, C. J.—A Practical Elementary Turkish Grammar. Crown 8vo, 6s.

TAYLOR, Rev. Isaac.—The Alphabet. An Account of the Origin and Development of Letters. With numerous Tables and Facsimiles. 2 vols. Demy 8vo, 36s.

TAYLOR, Jeremy.—The Marriage Ring. With Preface, Notes, and Appendices. Edited by FRANCIS BURDETT MONEY COUTTS. Small crown 8vo, 2s. 6d.

TAYLOR, Sedley. — Profit Sharing between Capital and Labour. To which is added a Memorandum on the Industrial Partnership at the Whitwood Collieries, by ARCHIBALD and HENRY BRIGGS, with remarks by SEDLEY TAYLOR. Crown 8vo, 2s. 6d.

THOM, J. Hamilton.—Laws of Life after the Mind of Christ. Two Series. Crown 8vo, 7*s.* 6*d.* each.

THOMPSON, Sir H.—Diet in Relation to Age and Activity. Fcap. 8vo, cloth, 1*s.* 6*d.* ; paper covers, 1*s.*

TIDMAN, Paul F.—Money and Labour. 1*s.* 6*d.*

TIPPLE, Rev. S. A.—Sunday Mornings at Norwood. Prayers and Sermons. Crown 8vo, 6*s.*

TODHUNTER, Dr. J.—A Study of Shelley. Crown 8vo, 7*s.*

TOLSTOI, Count Leo.—Christ's Christianity. Translated from the Russian. Large crown 8vo, 7*s.* 6*d.*

TRANT, William.—Trade Unions : Their Origin, Objects, and Efficacy. Small crown 8vo, 1*s.* 6*d.* ; paper covers, 1*s.*

TRENCH, The late R. C., Archbishop.—Notes on the Parables of Our Lord. Fourteenth Edition. 8vo, 12*s.* Cheap Edition, 7*s.* 6*d.*

Notes on the Miracles of Our Lord. Twelfth Edition. 8vo, 12*s.* Cheap Edition, 7*s.* 6*d.*

Studies in the Gospels. Fifth Edition, Revised. 8vo, 10*s.* 6*d.*

Brief Thoughts and Meditations on Some Passages in Holy Scripture. Third Edition. Crown 8vo, 3*s.* 6*d.*

Synonyms of the New Testament. Tenth Edition, Enlarged. 8vo, 12*s.*

Sermons New and Old. Crown 8vo, 6*s.*

On the Authorized Version of the New Testament. Second Edition. 8vo, 7*s.*

Commentary on the Epistles to the Seven Churches in Asia. Fourth Edition, Revised. 8vo, 8*s.* 6*d.*

The Sermon on the Mount. An Exposition drawn from the Writings of St. Augustine, with an Essay on his Merits as an Interpreter of Holy Scripture. Fourth Edition, Enlarged. 8vo, 10*s.* 6*d.*

Shipwrecks of Faith. Three Sermons preached before the University of Cambridge in May, 1867. Fcap. 8vo, 2*s.* 6*d.*

Lectures on Mediæval Church History. Being the Substance of Lectures delivered at Queen's College, London. Second Edition. 8vo, 12*s.*

English, Past and Present. Thirteenth Edition, Revised and Improved. Fcap. 8vo, 5*s.*

On the Study of Words. Nineteenth Edition, Revised. Fcap. 8vo, 5*s.*

TRENCH, The late R. C., Archbishop.—continued.

Select Glossary of English Words Used Formerly in Senses Different from the Present. Sixth Edition, Revised and Enlarged. Fcap. 8vo, 5*s.*

Proverbs and Their Lessons. Seventh Edition, Enlarged. Fcap. 8vo, 4*s.*

Poems. Collected and Arranged anew. Ninth Edition. Fcap. 8vo, 7*s.* 6*d.*

Poems. Library Edition. 2 vols. Small crown 8vo, 10*s.*

Sacred Latin Poetry. Chiefly Lyrical, Selected and Arranged for Use. Third Edition, Corrected and Improved. Fcap. 8vo, 7*s.*

A Household Book of English Poetry. Selected and Arranged, with Notes. Fourth Edition, Revised. Extra fcap. 8vo, 5*s.* 6*d.*

An Essay on the Life and Genius of Calderon. With Translations from his " Life's a Dream " and " Great Theatre of the World." Second Edition, Revised and Improved. Extra fcap. 8vo, 5*s.* 6*d.*

Gustavus Adolphus in Germany, and other Lectures on the Thirty Years' War. Third Edition, Enlarged. Fcap. 8vo, 4*s.*

Plutarch : his Life, his Lives, and his Morals. Second Edition, Enlarged. Fcap. 8vo, 3*s.* 6*d.*

Remains of the late Mrs. Richard Trench. Being Selections from her Journals, Letters, and other Papers. New and Cheaper Issue. With Portrait. 8vo, 6*s.*

TUKE, Daniel Hack, M.D., F.R.C.P.—**Chapters in the History of the Insane in the British Isles.** With Four Illustrations. Large crown 8vo, 12*s.*

TWINING, Louisa.—**Workhouse Visiting and Management during Twenty-Five Years.** Small crown 8vo, 2*s.*

VAUGHAN, H. Halford.—**New Readings and Renderings of Shakespeare's Tragedies.** 3 vols. Demy 8vo, 12*s.* 6*d.* each.

VICARY, J. Fulford.—**Saga Time.** With Illustrations. Crown 8vo, 7*s.* 6*d.*

VOGT, Lieut.-Col. Hermann.—**The Egyptian War of 1882.** A translation. With Map and Plans. Large crown 8vo, 6*s.*

VOLCKXSOM, E. W. v.—**Catechism of Elementary Modern Chemistry.** Small crown 8vo, 3*s.*

WALPOLE, Chas. George.—**A Short History of Ireland from the Earliest Times to the Union with Great Britain.** With 5 Maps and Appendices. Third Edition. Crown 8vo, 6*s.*

WARD, Wilfrid.—The Wish to Believe. A Discussion Concerning the Temper of Mind in which a reasonable Man should undertake Religious Inquiry. Small crown 8vo, 5*s.*

WARD, William George, Ph.D.—Essays on the Philosophy of Theism. Edited, with an Introduction, by WILFRID WARD. 2 vols. Demy 8vo, 21*s.*

WARNER, Francis, M.D.—Lectures on the Anatomy of Movement. Crown 8vo, 4*s.* 6*d.*

WARTER, J. W.—An Old Shropshire Oak. 2 vols. Demy 8vo, 28*s.*

WEDMORE, Frederick.—The Masters of Genre Painting. With Sixteen Illustrations. Post 8vo, 7*s.* 6*d.*

WHITMAN, Sidney.—Conventional Cant: its Results and Remedy. Crown 8vo, 6*s.*

WHITNEY, Prof. William Dwight.—Essentials of English Grammar, for the Use of Schools. Second Edition. Crown 8vo, 3*s.* 6*d.*

WHITWORTH, George Clifford.—An Anglo-Indian Dictionary : a Glossary of Indian Terms used in English, and of such English or other Non-Indian Terms as have obtained special meanings in India. Demy 8vo, cloth, 12*s.*

WILSON, Lieut.-Col. C. T.—The Duke of Berwick, Marshal of France, 1702-1734. Demy 8vo, 15*s.*

WILSON, Mrs. R. F.—The Christian Brothers. Their Origin and Work. With a Sketch of the Life of their Founder, the Ven. JEAN BAPTISTE, de la Salle. Crown 8vo, 6*s.*

WOLTMANN, Dr. Alfred, and WOERMANN, Dr. Karl.—History of Painting. With numerous Illustrations. Medium 8vo. Vol. I. Painting in Antiquity and the Middle Ages. 28*s.* ; bevelled boards, gilt leaves, 30*s.* Vol. II. The Painting of the Renascence. 42*s.* ; bevelled boards, gilt leaves, 45*s.*

YOUMANS, Edward L., M.D.—A Class Book of Chemistry, on the Basis of the New System. With 200 Illustrations. Crown 8vo, 5*s.*

YOUMANS, Eliza A.—First Book of Botany. Designed to Cultivate the Observing Powers of Children. With 300 Engravings. New and Cheaper Edition. Crown 8vo, 2*s.* 6*d.*

YOUNG, Arthur.—Axial Polarity of Man's Word-Embodied Ideas, and its Teaching. Demy 4to, 15*s.*

THE INTERNATIONAL SCIENTIFIC SERIES.

I. **Forms of Water in Clouds and Rivers, Ice and Glaciers.** By J. Tyndall, LL.D., F.R.S. With 25 Illustrations. Ninth Edition. 5*s*.

II. **Physics and Politics ;** or, Thoughts on the Application of the Principles of "Natural Selection" and "Inheritance" to Political Society. By Walter Bagehot. Eighth Edition. 4*s*.

III. **Foods.** By Edward Smith, M.D., LL.B., F.R.S. With numerous Illustrations. Ninth Edition. 5*s*.

IV. **Mind and Body :** the Theories and their Relation. By Alexander Bain, LL.D. With Four Illustrations. Eighth Edition. 4*s*.

V. **The Study of Sociology.** By Herbert Spencer. Thirteenth Edition. 5*s*.

VI. **On the Conservation of Energy.** By Balfour Stewart, M.A., LL.D., F.R.S. With 14 Illustrations. Seventh Edition. 5*s*.

VII. **Animal Locomotion ;** or Walking, Swimming, and Flying. By J. B. Pettigrew, M.D., F.R.S., etc. With 130 Illustrations. Third Edition. 5*s*.

VIII. **Responsibility in Mental Disease.** By Henry Maudsley, M.D. Fourth Edition. 5*s*.

IX. **The New Chemistry.** By Professor J. P. Cooke. With 31 Illustrations. Ninth Edition. 5*s*.

X. **The Science of Law.** By Professor Sheldon Amos. Sixth Edition. 5*s*.

XI. **Animal Mechanism :** a Treatise on Terrestrial and Aerial Locomotion. By Professor E. J. Marey. With 117 Illustrations. Third Edition. 5*s*.

XII. **The Doctrine of Descent and Darwinism.** By Professor Oscar Schmidt. With 26 Illustrations. Seventh Edition. 5*s*.

XIII. **The History of the Conflict between Religion and Science.** By J. W. Draper, M.D., LL.D. Twentieth Edition. 5*s*.

XIV. **Fungi :** their Nature, Influences, Uses, etc. By M. C. Cooke, M.D., LL.D. Edited by the Rev. M. J. Berkeley, M.A., F.L.S. With numerous Illustrations. Third Edition. 5*s*.

XV. **The Chemical Effects of Light and Photography.** By Dr. Hermann Vogel. With 100 Illustrations. Fourth Edition. 5*s*.

XVI. **The Life and Growth of Language.** By Professor William Dwight Whitney. Fifth Edition. 5*s*.

XVII. **Money and the Mechanism of Exchange.** By W Stanley Jevons, M.A., F.R.S. Eighth Edition. 5*s*.

XVIII. **The Nature of Light.** With a General Account of Physical Optics. By Dr. Eugene Lommel. With 188 Illustrations and a Table of Spectra in Chromo-lithography. Fourth Edition. 5*s*.

XIX. **Animal Parasites and Messmates.** By P. J. Van Beneden. With 83 Illustrations. Third Edition. 5*s*.

XX. **Fermentation.** By Professor Schützenberger. With 28 Illustrations. Fourth Edition. 5*s*.

XXI. **The Five Senses of Man.** By Professor Bernstein. With 91 Illustrations. Fifth Edition. 5*s*.

XXII. **The Theory of Sound in its Relation to Music.** By Professor Pietro Blaserna. With numerous Illustrations. Third Edition. 5*s*.

XXIII. **Studies in Spectrum Analysis.** By J. Norman Lockyer, F.R.S. With six photographic Illustrations of Spectra, and numerous engravings on Wood. Fourth Edition. 6*s*. 6*d*.

XXIV. **A History of the Growth of the Steam Engine.** By Professor R. H. Thurston. With numerous Illustrations. Fourth Edition. 6*s*. 6*d*.

XXV. **Education as a Science.** By Alexander Bain, LL.D. Sixth Edition. 5*s*.

XXVI. **The Human Species.** By Professor A. de Quatrefages. Fourth Edition. 5*s*.

XXVII. **Modern Chromatics.** With Applications to Art and Industry. By Ogden N. Rood. With 130 original Illustrations. Second Edition. 5*s*.

XXVIII. **The Crayfish** : an Introduction to the Study of Zoology. By Professor T. H. Huxley. With 82 Illustrations. Fourth Edition. 5*s*.

XXIX. **The Brain as an Organ of Mind.** By H. Charlton Bastian, M.D. With numerous Illustrations. Third Edition. 5*s*.

XXX. **The Atomic Theory.** By Prof. Wurtz. Translated by G. Cleminshaw, F.C.S. Fourth Edition. 5*s*.

XXXI. **The Natural Conditions of Existence as they affect Animal Life.** By Karl Semper. With 2 Maps and 106 Woodcuts. Third Edition. 5*s*.

XXXII. **General Physiology of Muscles and Nerves.** By Prof. J. Rosenthal. Third Edition. With Illustrations. 5*s*.

XXXIII. **Sight** : an Exposition of the Principles of Monocular and Binocular Vision. By Joseph le Conte, LL.D. Second Edition. With 132 Illustrations. 5*s*.

XXXIV. Illusions : a Psychological Study. By James Sully. Third Edition. 5*s.*

XXXV. Volcanoes : what they are and what they teach. By Professor J. W. Judd, F.R.S. With 92 Illustrations on Wood. Third Edition. 5*s.*

XXXVI. Suicide : an Essay on Comparative Moral Statistics. By Prof. H. Morselli. Second Edition. With Diagrams. 5*s.*

XXXVII. The Brain and its Functions. By J. Luys. With Illustrations. Second Edition. 5*s.*

XXXVIII. Myth and Science : an Essay. By Tito Vignoli. Third Edition. 5*s.*

XXXIX. The Sun. By Professor Young. With Illustrations. Second Edition. 5*s.*

XL. Ants, Bees, and Wasps : a Record of Observations on the Habits of the Social Hymenoptera. By Sir John Lubbock, Bart., M.P. With 5 Chromo-lithographic Illustrations. Eighth Edition. 5*s.*

XLI. Animal Intelligence. By G. J. Romanes, LL.D., F.R.S. Fourth Edition. 5*s.*

XLII. The Concepts and Theories of Modern Physics. By J. B. Stallo. Third Edition. 5*s.*

XLIII. Diseases of the Memory ; An Essay in the Positive Psycho-logy. By Prof. Th. Ribot. Third Edition. 5*s.*

XLIV. Man before Metals. By N. Joly, with 148 Illustrations. Fourth Edition. 5*s.*

XLV. The Science of Politics. By Prof. Sheldon Amos. Third Edition. 5*s.*

XLVI. Elementary Meteorology. By Robert H. Scott. Fourth Edition. With Numerous Illustrations. 5*s.*

XLVII. The Organs of Speech and their Application in the Formation of Articulate Sounds. By Georg Hermann Von Meyer. With 47 Woodcuts. 5*s.*

XLVIII. Fallacies. A View of Logic from the Practical Side. By Alfred Sidgwick. Second Edition. 5*s.*

XLIX. Origin of Cultivated Plants. By Alphonse de Candolle. 5*s.*

L. Jelly-Fish, Star-Fish, and Sea-Urchins. Being a Research on Primitive Nervous Systems. By G. J. Romanes. With Illustrations. 5*s.*

LI. The Common Sense of the Exact Sciences. By the late William Kingdon Clifford. Second Edition. With 100 Figures. 5*s.*

LII. **Physical Expression : Its Modes and Principles.** By Francis Warner, M.D., F.R.C.P., Hunterian Professor of Comparative Anatomy and Physiology, R.C.S.E. With 50 Illustrations. 5s.

LIII. **Anthropoid Apes.** By Robert Hartmann. With 63 Illustrations. 5s.

LIV. **The Mammalia in their Relation to Primeval Times.** By Oscar Schmidt. With 51 Woodcuts. 5s.

LV. **Comparative Literature.** By H. Macaulay Posnett, LL.D. 5s.

LVI. **Earthquakes and other Earth Movements.** By Prof. John Milne. With 38 Figures. Second Edition. 5s.

LVII. **Microbes, Ferments, and Moulds.** By E. L. Trouessart. With 107 Illustrations. 5s.

LVIII. **Geographical and Geological Distribution of Animals.** By Professor A. Heilprin. With Frontispiece. 5s.

LIX. **Weather.** A Popular Exposition of the Nature of Weather Changes from Day to Day. By the Hon. Ralph Abercromby. With 96 Illustrations. 5s.

LX. **Animal Magnetism.** By Alfred Binet and Charles Féré. 5s.

LXI. **Manual of British Discomycetes,** with descriptions of all the Species of Fungi hitherto found in Britain included in the Family, and Illustrations of the Genera. By William Phillips, F.L.S. 5s.

LXII. **International Law.** With Materials for a Code of International Law. By Professor Leoue Levi. 5s.

LXIII. **The Origin of Floral Structures through Insect Agency.** By Prof. G. Henslow.

MILITARY WORKS.

BRACKENBURY, Col. C. B., R.A. — **Military Handbooks for Regimental Officers.**

I. **Military Sketching and Reconnaissance.** By Col. F. J. Hutchison and Major H. G. MacGregor. Fifth Edition. With 15 Plates. Small crown 8vo, 4s.

II. **The Elements of Modern Tactics Practically applied to English Formations.** By Lieut.-Col. Wilkinson Shaw. Sixth Edition. With 25 Plates and Maps. Small crown 8vo, 9s.

III. **Field Artillery.** Its Equipment, Organization and Tactics. By Major Sisson C. Pratt, R.A. With 12 Plates. Third Edition. Small crown 8vo, 6s.

D

BRACKENBURY, Col. C. B., R.A.—continued.

IV. **The Elements of Military Administration.** First Part : Permanent System of Administration. By Major J. W. Buxton. Small crown 8vo, 7*s*. 6*d*.

V. **Military Law :** Its Procedure and Practice. By Major Sisson C. Pratt, R.A. Third Edition. Small crown 8vo, 4*s*. 6*d*.

VI. **Cavalry in Modern War.** By Col. F. Chenevix Trench. Small crown 8vo, 6*s*.

VII. **Field Works.** Their Technical Construction and Tactical Application. By the Editor, Col. C. B. Brackenbury, R.A. Small crown 8vo.

BRENT, Brig.-Gen. J. L.—**Mobilizable Fortifications and their Controlling Influence in War.** Crown 8vo, 5*s*.

BROOKE, Major, C. K.—**A System of Field Training.** Small crown 8vo, cloth limp, 2*s*.

Campaign of Fredericksburg, November—December, 1862. A Study for Officers of Volunteers. With 5 Maps and Plans. Crown 8vo, 5*s*.

CLERY, C., Lieut.-Col.—**Minor Tactics.** With 26 Maps and Plans. Seventh Edition, Revised. Crown 8vo, 9*s*.

COLVILE, Lieut. Col. C. F.—**Military Tribunals.** Sewed, 2*s*. 6*d*.

CRAUFURD, Capt. H. J.—**Suggestions for the Military Training of a Company of Infantry.** Crown 8vo, 1*s*. 6*d*.

HAMILTON, Capt. Ian, A.D.C.—**The Fighting of the Future.** 1*s*.

HARRISON, Col. R.—**The Officer's Memorandum Book for Peace and War.** Fourth Edition, Revised throughout. Oblong 32mo, red basil, with pencil, 3*s*. 6*d*.

Notes on Cavalry Tactics, Organisation, etc. By a Cavalry Officer. With Diagrams. Demy 8vo, 12*s*.

PARR, Capt. H. Hallam, C.M.G.—**The Dress, Horses, and Equipment of Infantry and Staff Officers.** Crown 8vo, 1*s*.

SCHAW, Col. H.—**The Defence and Attack of Positions and Localities.** Third Edition, Revised and Corrected. Crown 8vo, 3*s*. 6*d*.

STONE, Capt. F. Gleadowe, R.A.—**Tactical Studies from the Franco-German War of 1870-71.** With 22 Lithographic Sketches and Maps. Demy 8vo, 30*s*.

WILKINSON, H. Spenser, Capt. 20th Lancashire R.V. — **Citizen Soldiers.** Essays towards the Improvement of the Volunteer Force. Crown 8vo, 2*s*. 6*d*.

POETRY.

ABBAY, R.—The Castle of Knaresborough. A Tale in Verse. Crown 8vo, 6s.

ADAM OF ST. VICTOR.—The Liturgical Poetry of Adam of St. Victor. From the text of GAUTIER. With Translations into English in the Original Metres, and Short Explanatory Notes, by DIGBY S. WRANGHAM, M.A. 3 vols. Crown 8vo, printed on hand-made paper, boards, 21s.

AITCHISON, James.—The Chronicle of Mites. A Satire. Small crown 8vo. 5s.

ALEXANDER, William, D.D., Bishop of Derry.—St. Augustine's Holiday, and other Poems. Crown 8vo, 6s.

AUCHMUTY, A. C.—Poems of English Heroism : From Brunanburh to Lucknow; from Athelstan to Albert. Small crown 8vo, 1s. 6d.

BARNES, William.—Poems of Rural Life, in the Dorset Dialect. New Edition, complete in one vol. Crown 8vo, 8s. 6d.

BAYNES, Rev. Canon H. R.—Home Songs for Quiet Hours. Fourth and Cheaper Edition. Fcap. 8vo, cloth, 2s. 6d.

BEVINGTON, L. S.—Key Notes. Small crown 8vo, 5s.

BLUNT, Wilfrid Scawen. — The Wind and the. Whirlwind. Demy 8vo, 1s. 6d.

The Love Sonnets of Proteus. Fifth Edition, 18mo. Cloth extra, gilt top, 5s.

BOWEN, H. C., M.A.—Simple English Poems. English Literature for Junior Classes. In Four Parts. Parts I., II., and III., 6d. each, and Part IV., 1s. Complete, 3s.

BRYANT, W. C.—Poems. Cheap Edition, with Frontispiece. Small crown 8vo, 3s. 6d.

Calderon's Dramas : the Wonder-Working Magician — Life is a Dream—the Purgatory of St. Patrick. Translated by DENIS FLORENCE MACCARTHY. Post 8vo, 10s.

Camoens' Lusiads. — Portuguese Text, with Translation by J. J. AUBERTIN. Second Edition. 2 vols. Crown 8vo, 12s.

CAMPBELL, Lewis.—Sophocles. The Seven Plays in English Verse. Crown 8vo, 7s. 6d.

CERVANTES.—Journey to Parnassus. Spanish Text, with Translation into English Tercets, Preface, and Illustrative Notes, by JAMES Y. GIBSON. Crown 8vo, 12s.

CERVANTES—continued.

Numantia: a Tragedy. Translated from the Spanish, with Introduction and Notes, by JAMES Y. GIBSON. Crown 8vo, printed on hand-made paper, 5*s.*

Chronicles of Christopher Columbus. A Poem in 12 Cantos. By M. D. C. Crown 8vo, 7*s.* 6*d.*

Cid Ballads, and other Poems.—Translated from Spanish and German by J. Y. GIBSON. 2 vols. Crown 8vo, 12*s.*

COXHEAD, Ethel.—**Birds and Babies.** With 33 Illustrations. Imp. 16mo, gilt, 2*s.* 6*d.*

Dante's Divina Commedia. Translated in the *Terza Rima* of Original, by F. K. H. HASELFOOT. Demy 8vo, 16*s.*

DE BERANGER.—**A Selection from his Songs.** In English Verse. By WILLIAM TOYNBEE. Small crown 8vo, 2*s.* 6*d.*

DENNIS, J.—**English Sonnets.** Collected and Arranged by. Small crown 8vo, 2*s.* 6*d.*

DE VERE, Aubrey.—**Poetical Works.**

    I. THE SEARCH AFTER PROSERPÍNE, etc. 6*s.*
    II. THE LEGENDS OF ST. PATRICK, etc. 6*s.*
    III. ALEXANDER THE GREAT, etc. 6*s.*

    The Foray of Queen Meave, and other Legends of Ireland's Heroic Age. Small crown 8vo, 5*s.*

    Legends of the Saxon Saints. Small crown 8vo, 6*s.*

    Legends and Records of the Church and the Empire. Small crown 8vo, 6*s.*

DILLON, Arthur.—**Gods and Men.** Fcap. 4to, 7*s.* 6*d.*

DOBSON, Austin.—**Old World Idylls and other Verses.** Seventh Edition. Elzevir 8vo, gilt top, 6*s.*

    At the Sign of the Lyre. Fifth Edition. Elzevir 8vo, gilt top, 6*s.*

DOWDEN, Edward, LL.D.—**Shakspere's Sonnets.** With Introduction and Notes. Large post 8vo, 7*s.* 6*d.*

DUTT, Toru.—**A Sheaf Gleaned in French Fields.** New Edition. Demy 8vo, 10*s.* 6*d.*

    Ancient Ballads and Legends of Hindustan. With an Introductory Memoir by EDMUND GOSSE. Second Edition, 18mo. Cloth extra, gilt top, 5*s.*

EDWARDS, Miss Betham.—**Poems.** Small crown 8vo, 3*s.* 6*d.*

ELLIOTT, Ebenezer, The Corn Law Rhymer.—**Poems.** Edited by his son, the Rev. EDWIN ELLIOTT, of St. John's, Antigua. 2 vols. Crown 8vo, 18*s.*

English Verse. Edited by W. J. LINTON and R. H. STODDARD. 5 vols. Crown 8vo, cloth, 5*s.* each.
    I. CHAUCER TO BURNS.
    II. TRANSLATIONS.
    III. LYRICS OF THE NINETEENTH CENTURY.
    IV. DRAMATIC SCENES AND CHARACTERS.
    V. BALLADS AND ROMANCES.

FOSKETT, Edward.—**Poems.** Crown 8vo, 6*s.*

GOODCHILD, John A.—**Somnia Medici.** Three series. Small crown 8vo, 5*s.* each.

GOSSE, Edmund.—**New Poems.** Crown 8vo, 7*s.* 6*d.*

    Firdausi in Exile, and other Poems. Second Edition. Elzevir 8vo, gilt top, 6*s.*

GURNEY, Rev. Alfred.—**The Vision of the Eucharist,** and other Poems. Crown 8vo, 5*s.*

    A Christmas Faggot. Small crown 8vo, 5*s.*

HARRISON, Clifford.—**In Hours of Leisure.** Crown 8vo, 5*s.*

HEYWOOD, J. C.—**Herodias,** a Dramatic Poem. New Edition, Revised. Small crown 8vo, 5*s.*

    Antonius. A Dramatic Poem. New Edition, Revised. Small crown 8vo, 5*s.*

    Salome. A Dramatic Poem. Small crown 8vo, 5*s.*

HICKEY, E. H.—**A Sculptor,** and other Poems. Small crown 8vo, 5*s.*

HOLE, W. G.—**Procris,** and other Poems. Fcap. 8vo, 3*s.* 6*d.*

KEATS, John.—**Poetical Works.** Edited by W. T. ARNOLD. Large crown 8vo, choicely printed on hand-made paper, with Portrait in *eau-forte.* Parchment or cloth, 12*s.* ; vellum, 15*s.*

KING, Edward. **A Venetian Lover.** Small 4to, 6*s.*

KING, Mrs. Hamilton.—**The Disciples.** Ninth Edition, and Notes. Small crown 8vo, 5*s.*

    A Book of Dreams. Second Edition. Crown 8vo, 3*s.* 6*d.*

LAFFAN, Mrs. R. S. De Courcy.—**A Song of Jubilee, and other Poems.** With Frontispiece. Small crown 8vo, 3*s.* 6*d.*

LANG, A.—**XXXII. Ballades in Blue China.** Elzevir 8vo, 5*s.*

    Rhymes à la Mode. With Frontispiece by E. A. Abbey. Second Edition. Elzevir 8vo, cloth extra, gilt top, 5*s.*

LANGFORD, J. A., LL.D.—**On Sea and Shore.** Small crown 8vo, 5*s.*

LASCELLES, John.—Golden Fetters, and other Poems. Small crown 8vo, 3s. 6d.

LAWSON, Right Hon. Mr. Justice.—Hymni Usitati Latine Redditi : with other Verses. Small 8vo, parchment, 5s.

Living English Poets MDCCCLXXXII. With Frontispiece by Walter Crane. Second Edition. Large crown 8vo. Printed on hand-made paper. Parchment or cloth, 12s. ; vellum, 15s.

LOCKER, F.—London Lyrics. Tenth Edition. With Portrait, Elzevir 8vo. Cloth extra, gilt top, 5s.

Love in Idleness. A Volume of Poems. With an Etching by W. B. Scott. Small crown 8vo, 5s.

LUMSDEN, Lieut.-Col. H. W.—Beowulf : an Old English Poem. Translated into Modern Rhymes. Second and Revised Edition. Small crown 8vo, 5s.

LYSAGHT, Sidney Royse.—A Modern Ideal. A Dramatic Poem. Small crown 8vo, 5s.

MAGNUSSON, Eiríkr, M.A., and PALMER, E. H., M.A.—Johan Ludvig Runeberg's Lyrical Songs, Idylls, and Epigrams. Fcap. 8vo, 5s.

MEREDITH, Owen [The Earl of Lytton].—Lucile. New Edition. With 32 Illustrations. 16mo, 3s. 6d. Cloth extra, gilt edges, 4s. 6d.

MORRIS, Lewis.—Poetical Works of. New and Cheaper Editions, with Portrait. Complete in 3 vols., 5s. each.
Vol. I. contains "Songs of Two Worlds." Twelfth Edition.
Vol. II. contains "The Epic of Hades." Twenty-first Edition.
Vol. III. contains "Gwen" and "The Ode of Life." Seventh Edition.
Vol. IV. contains "Songs Unsung" and "Gycia." Fifth Edition.

Songs of Britain. Third Edition. Fcap. 8vo, 5s.

The Epic of Hades. With 16 Autotype Illustrations, after the Drawings of the late George R. Chapman. 4to, cloth extra, gilt leaves, 21s.

The Epic of Hades. Presentation Edition. 4to, cloth extra, gilt leaves, 10s. 6d.

The Lewis Morris Birthday Book. Edited by S. S. COPE-MAN, with Frontispiece after a Design by the late George R. Chapman. 32mo, cloth extra, gilt edges, 2s. ; cloth limp, 1s. 6d.

MORSHEAD, E. D. A. — The House of Atreus. Being the Agamemnon, Libation-Bearers, and Furies of Æschylus. Translated into English Verse. Crown 8vo, 7s.

The Suppliant Maidens of Æschylus. Crown 8vo, 3s. 6d.

MOZLEY, J. Rickards.—The Romance of Dennell. A Poem in Five Cantos. Crown 8vo, 7*s.* 6*d.*

MULHOLLAND, Rosa.—Vagrant Verses. Small crown 8vo, 5*s.*

NADEN, Constance C. W.—A Modern Apostle, and other Poems. Small crown 8vo, 5*s.*

NOEL, The Hon. Roden.—A Little Child's Monument. Third Edition. Small crown 8vo, 3*s.* 6*d.*

The House of Ravensburg. New Edition. Small crown 8vo, 6*s.*

The Red Flag, and other Poems. New Edition. Small crown 8vo, 6*s.*

Songs of the Heights and Deeps. Crown 8vo, 6*s.*

O'BRIEN, Charlotte Grace.—Lyrics. Small crown 8vo, 3*s.* 6*d.*

O'HAGAN, John.—The Song of Roland. Translated into English Verse. New and Cheaper Edition. Crown 8vo, 5*s.*

PFEIFFER, Emily.—The Rhyme of the Lady of the Rock, and How it Grew. Second Edition. Small crown 8vo, 3*s.* 6*d.*

Gerard's Monument, and other Poems. Second Edition. Crown 8vo, 6*s.*

Under the Aspens: Lyrical and Dramatic. With Portrait. Crown 8vo, 6*s.*

PIATT, J. J.—Idyls and Lyrics of the Ohio Valley. Crown 8vo, 5*s.*

PREVOST, Francis.—Melilot. 3*s.* 6*d.*

Fires of Green Wood. Small crown 8vo, 3*s.* 6*d.*

Rare Poems of the 16th and 17th Centuries. Edited by W. J. LINTON. Crown 8vo, 5*s.*

RHOADES, James.—The Georgics of Virgil. Translated into English Verse. Small crown 8vo, 5*s.*

Poems. Small crown 8vo, 4*s.* 6*d.*

Dux Redux. A Forest Tangle. Small crown 8vo, 3*s.* 6*d.*

ROBINSON, A. Mary F.—A Handful of Honeysuckle. Fcap. 8vo, 3*s.* 6*d.*

The Crowned Hippolytus. Translated from Euripides. With New Poems. Small crown 8vo, 5*s.*

SCHILLER, Friedrich.—Wallenstein. A Drama. Done in English Verse, by J. A. W. HUNTER, M.A. Crown 8vo, 7*s.* 6*d.*

SCHWARTZ, J. M. W.—Nivalis. A Tragedy in Five Acts. Small crown 8vo, 5*s.*

SCOTT, E. J. L.—The Eclogues of Virgil.—Translated into English Verse. Small crown 8vo, 3*s.* 6*d.*

SHERBROOKE, Viscount.—Poems of a Life. Second Edition. Small crown 8vo, 2*s.* 6*d.*

SINCLAIR, Julian.—Nakiketas, and other Poems. Small crown 8vo, 2*s.* 6*d.*

SMITH, J. W. Gilbart.—The Loves of Vandyck. A Tale of Genoa. Small crown 8vo, 2*s.* 6*d.*

The Log o' the "Norseman." Small crown 8vo, 5*s.*

Serbelloni. Small crown 8vo, 5*s.*

Sophocles : The Seven Plays in English Verse. Translated by LEWIS CAMPBELL. Crown 8vo, 7*s.* 6*d.*

STEWART, Phillips.—Poems. Small crown 8vo, 2*s.* 6*d.*

SYMONDS, John Addington.—Vagabunduli Libellus. Crown 8vo, 6*s.*

Tasso's Jerusalem Delivered. Translated by Sir JOHN KINGSTON JAMES, Bart. Two Volumes. Printed on hand-made paper, parchment, bevelled boards. Large crown 8vo, 21*s.*

TAYLOR, Sir H.—Works. Complete in Five Volumes. Crown 8vo, 30*s.*

Philip Van Artevelde. Fcap. 8vo, 3*s.* 6*d.*

The Virgin Widow, etc. Fcap. 8vo, 3*s.* 6*d.*

The Statesman. Fcap. 8vo, 3*s.* 6*d.*

TODHUNTER, Dr. J.—Laurella, and other Poems. Crown 8vo, 6*s.* 6*d.*

Forest Songs. Small crown 8vo, 3*s.* 6*d.*

The True Tragedy of Rienzi : a Drama. 3*s.* 6*d.*

Alcestis : a Dramatic Poem. Extra fcap. 8vo, 5*s.*

Helena in Troas. Small crown 8vo, 2*s.* 6*d.*

TOMKINS, Zitella E.—Sister Lucetta, and other Poems. Small crown 8vo, 3*s.* 6*d.*

TYNAN, Katherine.—Louise de la Vallière, and other Poems. Small crown 8vo, 3*s.* 6*d.*

Shamrocks. Small crown 8vo, 5*s.*

Unspoken Thoughts. Small crown 8vo, 3*s.* 6*d.*

Victorian Hymns : English Sacred Songs of Fifty Years. Dedicated to the Queen. Large post 8vo, 10*s.* 6*d.*

WEBSTER, Augusta.—In a Day : a Drama. Small crown 8vo, 2*s.* 6*d.*

Disguises : a Drama. Small crown 8vo, 5*s.*

WILLIAMS, James.—A Lawyer's Leisure. Small crown 8vo, 3*s.* 6*d.*

WOOD, Edmund.—Poems. Small crown 8vo, 3*s.* 6*d.*

Wordsworth Birthday Book, The. Edited by ADELAIDE and VIOLET WORDSWORTH. 32mo, limp cloth, 1*s.* 6*d.* ; cloth extra, 2*s.*

YOUNGS, Ella Sharpe.—Paphus, and other Poems. Small crown 8vo, 3*s.* 6*d.*

A Heart's Life, Sarpedon, and other Poems. Small crown 8vo, 5*s.* 6*d.*

The Apotheosis of Antinous, and other Poems. With Portrait. Small crown 8vo, 10*s.* 6*d.*

NOVELS AND TALES.

" All But : " a Chronicle of Laxenford Life. By PEN OLIVER, F.R.C.S. With 20 Illustrations. Second Edition. Crown 8vo, 6*s.*

BANKS, Mrs. G. L.—God's Providence House. New Edition. Crown 8vo, 3*s.* 6*d.*

CHICHELE, Mary.—Doing and Undoing. A Story. Crown 8vo, 4*s.* 6*d.*

Danish Parsonage. By an Angler. Crown 8vo, 6*s.*

GRAY, Maxwell. — The Silence of Dean Maitland. Fifth Edition. With Frontispiece. Crown 8vo, 6*s.*

HUNTER, Hay.—The Crime of Christmas Day. A Tale of the Latin Quarter. By the Author of "My Ducats and my Daughter." 1*s.*

HUNTER, Hay, and WHYTE, Walter.—My Ducats and My Daughter. New and Cheaper Edition. With Frontispiece. Crown 8vo, 6*s.*

INGELOW, Jean.—Off the Skelligs : a Novel. With Frontispiece. Second Edition. Crown 8vo, 6*s.*

JENKINS, Edward.—A Secret of Two Lives. Crown 8vo, 2*s.* 6*d.*

KIELLAND, Alexander L.—Garman and Worse. A Norwegian Novel. Authorized Translation, by W. W. Kettlewell. Crown 8vo, 6*s.*

LANG, Andrew.—In the Wrong Paradise, and other Stories. Second Edition. Crown 8vo, 6*s.*

MACDONALD, G.—Donal Grant. A Novel. Second Edition. With Frontispiece. Crown 8vo, 6*s.*

Home Again. With Frontispiece. Crown 8vo, 6*s.*

Castle Warlock. A Novel. Second Edition. With Frontispiece. Crown 8vo, 6*s.*

MACDONALD, G.—continued.

Malcolm. With Portrait of the Author engraved on Steel. Eighth Edition. Crown 8vo, 6*s*.

The Marquis of Lossie. Seventh Edition. With Frontispiece. Crown 8vo, 6*s*.

St. George and St. Michael. Fifth Edition. With Frontispiece. Crown 8vo, 6*s*.

What's Mine's Mine. Second Edition. With Frontispiece. Crown 8vo, 6*s*.

Annals of a Quiet Neighbourhood. Sixth Edition. With Frontispiece. Crown 8vo, 6*s*.

The Seaboard Parish : a Sequel to "Annals of a Quiet Neighbourhood." Fourth Edition. With Frontispiece. Crown 8vo, 6*s*.

Wilfred Cumbermede. An Autobiographical Story. Fourth Edition. With Frontispiece. Crown 8vo, 6*s*.

Thomas Wingfold, Curate. Fourth Edition. With Frontispiece. Crown 8vo, 6*s*.

Paul Faber, Surgeon. Fourth Edition. With Frontispiece. Crown 8vo, 6*s*.

MALET, Lucas.—**Colonel Enderby's Wife.** A Novel. New and Cheaper Edition. With Frontispiece. Crown 8vo, 6*s*.

MULHOLLAND, Rosa.—**Marcella Grace.** An Irish Novel. Crown 8vo, 6*s*.

PALGRAVE, W. Gifford.—**Hermann Agha :** an Eastern Narrative. Third Edition. Crown 8vo, 6*s*.

SHAW, Flora L.—**Castle Blair :** a Story of Youthful Days. New and Cheaper Edition. Crown 8vo, 3*s*. 6*d*.

STRETTON, Hesba.—**Through a Needle's Eye :** a Story. New and Cheaper Edition, with Frontispiece. Crown 8vo, 6*s*.

TAYLOR, Col. Meadows, C.S.I., M.R.I.A.—**Seeta :** a Novel. With Frontispiece. Crown 8vo, 6*s*.

Tippoo Sultaun : a Tale of the Mysore War. With Frontispiece. Crown 8vo, 6*s*.

Ralph Darnell. With Frontispiece. Crown 8vo, 6*s*.

A Noble Queen. With Frontispiece. Crown 8vo, 6*s*.

The Confessions of a Thug. With Frontispiece. Crown 8vo, 6*s*.

Tara : a Mahratta Tale. With Frontispiece. Crown 8vo, 6*s*.

Within Sound of the Sea. With Frontispiece. Crown 8vo, 6*s*.

BOOKS FOR THE YOUNG.

Brave Men's Footsteps. A Book of Example and Anecdote for Young People. By the Editor of "Men who have Risen." With 4 Illustrations by C. Doyle. Ninth Edition. Crown 8vo, 3*s.* 6*d.*

COXHEAD, Ethel.—**Birds and Babies.** With 33 Illustrations. Second Edition. Imp. 16mo, cloth gilt, 2*s.* 6*d.*

DAVIES, G. Christopher.—**Rambles and Adventures of our School Field Club.** With 4 Illustrations. New and Cheaper Edition. Crown 8vo, 3*s.* 6*d.*

EDMONDS, Herbert.—**Well Spent Lives :** a Series of Modern Biographies. New and Cheaper Edition. Crown 8vo, 3*s.* 6*d.*

EVANS, Mark.—**The Story of our Father's Love,** told to Children. Sixth and Cheaper Edition of Theology for Children. With 4 Illustrations. Fcap. 8vo, 1*s.* 6*d.*

MAC KENNA, S. J.—**Plucky Fellows.** A Book for Boys. With 6 Illustrations. Fifth Edition. Crown 8vo, 3*s.* 6*d.*

MALET, Lucas.—**Little Peter.** A Christmas Morality for Children of any Age. With numerous Illustrations. 5*s.*

REANEY, Mrs. G. S.—**Waking and Working ;** or, From Girlhood to Womanhood. New and Cheaper Edition. With a Frontispiece. Crown 8vo, 3*s.* 6*d.*

Blessing and Blessed : a Sketch of Girl Life. New and Cheaper Edition. Crown 8vo, 3*s.* 6*d.*

Rose Gurney's Discovery. A Story for Girls. Dedicated to their Mothers. Crown 8vo, 3*s.* 6*d.*

English Girls : Their Place and Power. With Preface by the Rev. R. W. Dale. Fifth Edition. Fcap. 8vo, 2*s.* 6*d.*

Just Anyone, and other Stories. Three Illustrations. Royal 16mo, 1*s.* 6*d.*

Sunbeam Willie, and other Stories. Three Illustrations. Royal 16mo, 1*s.* 6*d.*

Sunshine Jenny, and other Stories. Three Illustrations. Royal 16mo, 1*s.* 6*d.*

STORR, Francis, and TURNER, Hawes.—**Canterbury Chimes ;** or, Chaucer Tales re-told to Children. With 6 Illustrations from the Ellesmere Manuscript. Third Edition. Fcap. 8vo, 3*s.* 6*d.*

STRETTON, Hesba.—**David Lloyd's Last Will.** With 4 Illustrations. New Edition. Royal 16mo, 2*s.* 6*d.*

WHITAKER, Florence.—**Christy's Inheritance.** A London Story. Illustrated. Royal 16mo, 1*s.* 6*d.*

MESSRS.

KEGAN PAUL, TRENCH & CO.'S

EDITIONS OF

SHAKSPERE'S WORKS.

THE PARCHMENT LIBRARY EDITION.

THE AVON EDITION.

The Text of these Editions is mainly that of Delius. Wherever a variant reading is adopted, some good and recognized Shaksperian Critic has been followed. In no case is a new rendering of the text proposed; nor has it been thought necessary to distract the reader's attention by notes or comments.

1, PATERNOSTER SQUARE.

[P. T. O.

SHAKSPERE'S WORKS.

THE AVON EDITION.

Printed on thin opaque paper, and forming 12 handy volumes, cloth, 18*s.*, or bound in 6 volumes, 15*s.*

The set of 12 volumes may also be had in a cloth box, price 21*s.*, or bound in Roan, Persian, Crushed Persian Levant, Calf, or Morocco, and enclosed in an attractive leather box at prices from 31*s.* 6*d.* upwards.

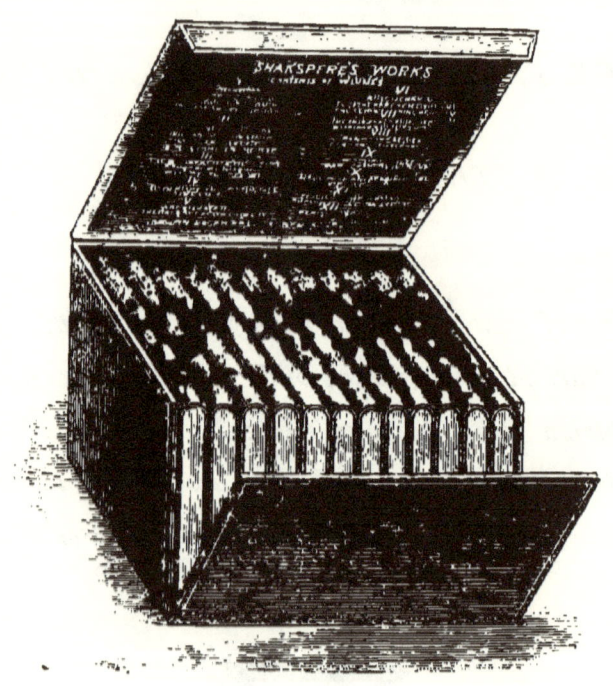

SOME PRESS NOTICES.

SHAKSPERE'S WORKS.

THE PARCHMENT LIBRARY EDITION.

In 12 volumes Elzevir 8vo., choicely printed on hand-made paper, and bound in parchment or cloth, price £3 12s., or in vellum, price £4 10s.

The set of 12 volumes may also be had in a strong cloth box, price £3 17s., or with an oak hanging shelf, £3 18s.

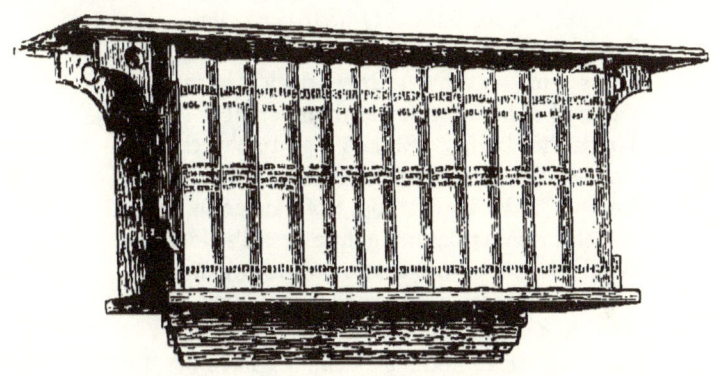

SOME PRESS NOTICES.

". . . There is, perhaps, no edition in which the works of Shakspere can be read in such luxury of type and quiet distinction of form as this, and we warmly recommend it."—*Pall Mall Gazette.*

"For elegance of form and beauty of typography, no edition of Shakspere hitherto published has excelled the 'Parchment Library Edition.' . . . They are in the strictest sense pocket volumes, yet the type is bold, and, being on fine white hand-made paper, can hardly tax the weakest of sight. The print is judiciously confined to the text, notes being more appropriate to library editions. The whole will be comprised in the cream-coloured parchment which gives the name to the series."—*Daily News.*

"The Parchment Library Edition of Shakspere needs no further praise."—*Saturday Review.*

Just published. Price 5s.

AN INDEX TO THE WORKS OF SHAKSPERE.

Applicable to all editions of Shakspere, and giving reference, by topics, to notable passages and significant expressions; brief histories of the plays; geographical names and historic incidents; mention of all characters and sketches of important ones; together with explanations of allusions and obscure and obsolete words and phrases.

By EVANGELINE M. O'CONNOR.

LONDON : KEGAN PAUL, TRENCH & CO., 1, PATERNOSTER SQUARE.

SHAKSPERE'S WORKS.

SPECIMEN OF TYPE.

Salar.   My wind, cooling my broth,
Would blow me to an ague, when I thought
What harm a wind too great might do at sea.
I should not see the sandy hour-glass run
But I should think of shallows and of flats,
And see my wealthy Andrew, dock'd in sand,
Vailing her high-top lower than her ribs
To kiss her burial.   Should I go to church
And see the holy edifice of stone,
And not bethink me straight of dangerous rocks,
Which touching but my gentle vessel's side,
Would scatter all her spices on the stream,
Enrobe the roaring waters with my silks,
And, in a word, but even now worth this,
And now worth nothing?   Shall I have the thought
To think on this, and shall I lack the thought
That such a thing bechanc'd would make me sad?
But tell not me : I know Antonio
Is sad to think upon his merchandise.

Ant. Believe me, no : I thank my fortune for it,
My ventures are not in one bottom trusted,
Nor to one place; nor is my whole estate
Upon the fortune of this present year :
Therefore my merchandise makes me not sad.

Salar. Why, then you are in love.

Ant.   Fie, fie!

Salar. Not in love neither?   Then let us say you
     are sad,
Because you are not merry; and 'twere as easy
For you to laugh, and leap, and say you are merry,
Because you are not sad.   Now, by two-headed
     Janus,
Nature hath fram'd strange fellows in her time :
Some that will evermore peep through their eyes
And laugh like parrots at a bag-piper;
And other of such vinegar aspect

www.ingramcontent.com/pod-product-compliance
Lightning Source LLC
Chambersburg PA
CBHW020612030726
47497CB00007B/2206